THE SHERPA
AND OTHER FICTIONS

THE SHERPA

AND OTHER FICTIONS

*To Khaiam,
On all our journeys
may peace find us
there*

NILA GUPTA

SUMACH
PRESS

LIBRARY AND ARCHIVES CANADA CATALOGUING IN PUBLICATION

Gupta, Nila
The Sherpa and other fictions / Nila Gupta.

ISBN 978-1-894549-70-7

I. Title.

PS8613.U685S47 2008   C813'.6   C2008-901240-2

Edited by Jennifer Day
Cover and design by Elizabeth Martin

*Sumach Press acknowledges the support of the Canada Council
for the Arts and the Ontario Arts Council for our publishing program.
We acknowledge the financial support of the Government of Canada
through the Book Publishing Industry Development Program
(BPIDP) for our publishing activities.*

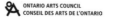 ONTARIO ARTS COUNCIL
CONSEIL DES ARTS DE L'ONTARIO

Printed and bound in Canada

Published by

SUMACH PRESS
1415 Bathurst Street #202
Toronto Canada
M5R 3H8
info@sumachpress.com
www.sumachpress.com

DEDICATION

For my father, who never left.

ACKNOWLEDGEMENTS

I am incredibly grateful to the K.M. Hunter Foundation, through the auspices of the Ontario Arts Council, for awarding me the K.M. Hunter Artists Award for Literature in 2004, and to the Toronto Arts Council and the Ontario Arts Council whose financial support allowed me to cocoon in myself in my writing room and play with words and worlds. I am also grateful to Marion Hebb and Sally Cohen of Marion Hebb & Associates, my legal representatives, who shepherded me through the business side of the publishing world and made sure I found a good home for my book.

Thanks to all my many teachers along the way: Guillermo Verdecchia, Ken Chubb, Ingrid MacDonald, Nourbese Philip, who each taught me something different about story structure, and Cynthia Holz, who enthusiastically critiqued early drafts of a number of the stories in this book and guided me through the process of sending out my manuscript to publishers. I am indebted to my good friends and fellow writers, Carolyn Black and Claudia Bickel, who read and critiqued draft versions of my manuscript. Their faith in me, and their unwavering attention to detail and honest responses made all the difference. Thanks to my dedicated reader, Nadia Kurd, who checked my facts about Kashmir and made sure I got things right. Much appreciation to the talented and eagle-eyed professors at the University of Guelph-Humber MFA in Creative Writing program, especially Dionne Brand, Michael Helm, Thomas King, and my mentor, Anita Rau Badami, whose attention to language and line was invaluable to my growth as a writer. And a heartfelt thanks to all the good-hearted staff at Sumach Press who were a pleasure to work with, and especially to Jennifer Day, my editor, who somehow managed to cajole me into revisiting even my most cherished passages.

Last, but not least, praise is due Natalie Wood, the first reader to each and every piece of writing and a loving incubator of even my wildest ideas and most bizarre fantasies.

The title story, "The Sherpa," was first published in *Descant*, Fall 2007.

CONTENTS

❦ THE SHERPA

IN ANOTHER LIFE, MY UNCLE, MAKHAN CHAND, MUST HAVE BEEN A Sherpa woman. The way he sweeps his arm in the Sherpa's direction as if he means to sweep all the dust of the Himalayas away, to clear our vision so we may see her through the grime, the mire, the vomit-flecked window of this bus we ride on our way to Mansar Lake.

The Sherpa outside our window is a bent old woman wearing trousers, walking slowly uphill, carrying a load of thick branches on her head. Her face is a deeply lined walnut, her eyes slits to the searing afternoon sun, the blowing sand, the black exhaust clouds that puff out the backsides of tin buses. In her hand she waves a stick she uses to guide her black goats and tan-coloured sheep along this zigzagging road that scratches its way up the face of the Himalayas, scarring it. She is used to navigating the many tiny footpaths that goat, sheep and Sherpa have trod in search of scrub. She is used to sharing this road with drivers who barely slow to pass, rarely slow to take the hairpin turns. Their only courtesy, one offered after they pass her, a belligerent honking of horn.

"Look how hard her life is," Makhan Chand says to his daughter Prithi and me, sitting snug in our seats. Our passing bus has just shrouded the Sherpa in black soot. Makhan Chand's face is puckered with grief, as if the Sherpa's suffering is his very own. He means to awaken us to her lot. I am impressed with my uncle, at what he can see, how he can call forth a living, breathing, toiling woman out of dust.

I am suddenly moved, almost enough to tell him about my life, just to feel the warmth of his all-seeing eyes on me, to hear him say, "How hard your life has been, how you've suffered."

My attention snarls in childhood memories of similar day jaunts to Mansar Lake. The bus station where we boarded is still a huge, open-air field of coughing, belching, bucking buses straining under the weight of parcels, luggage, furniture strapped on their roofs. Inside the bus, villagers with sacks of rice, lentils and peas balanced on their heads still jostle for space with tourists, camera straps slung over their shoulders. The nervous young men, though, are new, on their way to the trouble in Kashmir, clad in olive green fatigues and girdled with ammo belts. They clatter against each other, their eyes skittish, hands tight around water canisters, guns clenched against their bellies as if to protect against theft.

My cousin Prithi, in her gauzy grey *dupatta* and dull brown *salwar kameez,* and I, in shocking pink pants and emerald green University of Toronto sweatshirt, are lucky to find seats on this overcrowded bus. Makhan Chand's reproving look to two schoolboys had them springing up to offer us their hard metal seats. Makhan Chand looks like every village headmaster I have ever imagined, though when I was small, my teachers wore black robes and white habits and, once each month, kept their palms open to receive my father's rupees.

As the view slips by me I think of my father. The heaviness of what he has carried in his back pocket, the weight of an airplane he never flew back to India. His tilt against air currents that kept him from drifting India-ward, keeping me away too until I waded across the tarmac for a flight of my own. In my pockets, kept safe all these years, hope wrapped in yellow cloth, hope of what a woman might offer, a welcoming lap swathed in slippery softness, a yellow sari, flowing like waves under my hands. I can almost visualize that reunion, where longing meets reality. The home of Madame Jaune, a whitewashed bungalow with a wide verandah and a wooden screen door. The front and side gardens are abloom in roses even in seasons of water shortages. She is on the verandah awaiting my arrival with her arms flung around herself in the pose of happiness.

There is only one way out of the dusty arid side of the Himalayas and we are climbing up its steep face to the tunnel that opens into the lush valley of Kashmir. I feel the climb first in my body, the way I am pushed back into my seat, the face of the bus pointed skyward as if it means to take flight. The cursing, red-eyed driver navigates around pony carts and their slippery trail of fallen apples, skirts around heaps of rocks, around deep depressions in the road, all an inch away from the edge with no fence. The young soldiers, unaccustomed to being held to the walls of the mountain only by the thin metal of a rickety bus, unaccustomed to the view of a sheer, endless vertical drop, gulp for air, their heads hanging out the window. Makhan Chand smiles at me reassuringly.

Makhan Chand is my Aunt Puspha's husband, a former desk-sitting Indian civil servant, now retired. His white Nehru cap sits on a shock of white hair that he wears cut close to the scalp, a brush cut. His skin is a paprika brown, glowing with health, and though he is old, his back is ramrod straight. On our return from Mansar Lake, he disembarks from the bus and walks swiftly, just as he did around the perimeter of the lake, his hands clasped behind his back. He is used to leading the way, a man used to keeping appointments. I have to scurry to keep up. My cousin Prithi glides one step behind, arms folded in front of her chest, lost in thought, as gauzy as the *dupatta* that floats behind her in the breeze.

In Ragunath, the business section of town, the shops are linked wooden cubes, two rooms deep, raised a few feet above ground as a protection against floods. A multitude of hand-painted signs bear my family name. Makhan Chand introduces me to the sari shop owner, the dry goods shopkeeper, the photographer, the jeweller.

"Do you remember them?" Makhan Chand asks.

The men smile hopefully.

I shrug apologetically.

Makhan Chand pats my shoulder, "So little when you left." He then points to each in turn. "This is your father's brother's wife's uncle. This is your father's sister's husband's sister's husband."

It seems to me that I am related to everyone by blood or marriage and my head is spinning to keep up with the complex relations and unfamiliar terms. I am introduced as his wife's brother's daughter. Shiv's daughter, his niece from Canada, now returned.

"Ah, Shiv, BSc," the older ones nod and laugh, conjuring up the image of my father, a thin, driven, ambitious young man with bad teeth, who finished his BSc and went abroad, just as the astrologer predicted. Everywhere I go, they call him "Shiv, BSc" In this sleepy hill town, they seem so amazed by the accomplishment of a BSc I don't bother to tell them that my father has a PhD, too.

The first time I saw my father cry was at the airport. I was buying an insurance policy in case the plane crashed. I told him that I had made him the beneficiary. He told me, "Don't tell them I've lost my job. Don't tell them about your mother. Don't tell them you don't live at home. For once, behave as if you were my daughter."

My father holds two PhDs and speaks six languages: Dogri, his ancestral tongue; Hindi, India's official language; Urdu and Punjabi, as nods to his neighbours; English and French, the language of his PhD and of my mercurial mother, a woman he met while studying at the University of Montreal. Yet my father is afraid, in any language, of simple questions: questions well-meaning, homesick strangers or nodding acquaintances might ask on bumping shopping carts at Knob Hill Farms: "How is work? How is wife keeping? How are children doing?"

My father's dreams of winning the Nobel Prize in microbiology have been placed in deep freeze, waiting for better times. After the university laboratory where he worked was privatized, my father developed the vaccines the new laboratory owners wanted him to make; he, a Hindu, developed the vaccines for cows to keep them healthy until slaughter. The new CEO downsized him anyway.

I am my father's errant, runaway daughter. My hair is a tangled mess, cut short, one earring dangles out of my left ear. In the other ear, my father's litany, like children's marbles worrying each other in a pouch: "In India, children study all-day, even during vacations. In India, girls do not look at boys. In India, only the hippies wear jeans, take drugs and go to parties. In India, people love their culture. In India, people are happy." But my father's not pleased that I'm returning to India. He's afraid of what my delinquent tongue might drop before my relatives.

We are deep in the ancient walled city of narrow, winding cobblestone streets lined on both sides by high stone walls and open gutters, clear water streaming through. This city is clean, though my feet have to be on the lookout for dung dropped by the old, white knights, the emaciated cows that wander the streets, the humps of their bones jutting out. Every few metres, stone steps lead up to an open doorway, and Makhan Chand stops to greet strangers, his friends and neighbours alike. "Bapu-ji! Bapu-ji!" *Father*. Children rush to lay their soft cheeks into the soft cup of his hands, to feel the warmth of his gaze. "Beta. Beti." *Son. Daughter*. Makhan Chand responds equally to each in turn.

Makhan Chand's home, within the stone walls, is made up of a few rooms that ring an open air courtyard for cooking and sunning one's hair dry. On the roof is the latrine, kept clean by a sweeper who comes by each morning to empty out the pail. In the spartan room that Prithi shares with her mother, we sit cross-legged on the wooden bench that doubles as a bed, the soft, cotton-covered mattress rolled up on one end. Prithi turns over a cardboard box. Photographs drift out, black and white confetti. My Aunt Puspha sniffs softly in the kitchen, rolling chapathis for the evening's supper. Every once in a while, she comes into the room to stare at me, her hands ghostly, gloved with white flour. Her eyes are soft and grey with cataracts. Makhan Chand has gone to get *ras malai*, *burfi* and *gulab jamuns* from the sweet shop his brother's wife's brother owns, in celebration of my arrival.

"This is my sister, Radha," Prithi points to a studio photograph of a young woman, just out of her teens, her eyes lined with kohl. In this picture, she is pitched forward, her arms clasping each other beneath her *dupatta*, a huge smile on her excited face. She looks like she is about to burst into laughter, sparking to her own delight. Though Prithi doesn't remark on it, of all the photos of my relatives I've seen so far, Radha resembles me the most. Not the happiness, but the facial features; the long hooked nose I share with my father, the high forehead, the cat's eyes, deep-set and angled up at the corner.

"This is my brother, Dinesh," Prithi cups the photo gently in her hands, and then with a wistful smile, passes it to me. Dinesh is movie star handsome, a self-assured, well-fed young man in a tight, sleeveless wool vest and white shirt. A lopsided grin breaks open the secrets of his face. He looks like my father used to in photographs I have seen of him before he came to Canada, buoyant and satisfied.

It is underwater quiet in this stone enclosure. I hear the faraway cries of excited children. I hear the soft rustle of Prithi's *salwar kameez* as she turns photographs over and gives names to the faces that smile, squint and frown at me. In the open courtyard, there is a string cot that I know will soon lure my still jet-lagged body into its web for a rest. I wonder if I'll meet Prithi's siblings, Radha and Dinesh, my surprise cousins, later. In the rough genealogy tree my father sketched on the back of an airport restaurant napkin, Prithi is an only child. I'm perturbed that my father has not mentioned her siblings to me, and just as I have, has seemingly forgotten them.

"You will not keep this from me, too," I had rehearsed on the long wormhole subway ride to Kennedy Station, my ire rising with each passing station. I charged into the tree-lined suburbs, ready to pry information loose from my tight-fisted father, to ransack his house, if necessary, to find the addresses of my relatives in India. When I entered the house, my father was in the disheveled kitchen making *matter panir* for me, stirring the pot disarmingly. He didn't say yes, and he didn't say no. "It's late. Stay the night. We can talk in the morning. Have some tea."

I played with my dog, Lucky, in the backyard, under the harsh spotlight of the backdoor light. I threw a tennis ball for him until, finally, he tired. I felt sorry for my dog, sorry that I had to leave him behind in all my running away. Sorry for the way he still cowered and simpered around my father, his tail between his legs, cautiously inching forward for a pat, despite the kicks my father aims at his stomach.

In the morning, ambushed by both parents, I protested from under pink sheets, "But I'm naked!" They didn't run out of the room in horror to allow me my privacy. Instead, arms crossed over chests, blocking the door, they were determined to talk sense into me. I squirmed in my old bed. Lucky was of no help, cringing in the presence of my father in the corner of my room, under my dusty study table.

My mother and father, divided usually, were united fronts, inflated air bags, plump and satisfied with their job well done, trapping me. "It's not safe for girls to travel alone in India. It's just not done. There's trouble in the Punjab. There's trouble in Kashmir." My nakedness disarmed even me. I couldn't get up the courage to leap out of bed and stamp my foot at them.

"Daddy?" I said instead. "How come we never *ever* went back to India, like other families?"

My father contracted under my gaze. He had no answer, his desire for return frozen deep in the liquid nitrogen he used to use at his lab.

My mother advanced on my bed. "If you're going to go, then …" She reached for my hair, a pair of scissors glinted by my face. For a moment, I recoiled. "For the DNA, in case anyone murders you and puts an impostor in your place," she explained. It's how she's been thinking ever since my older brother smashed his car into a light standard on the rolling hills of the Don Valley Parkway, splitting his gangly teenage body and the family sedan in two. It's how she's been thinking since what followed: the other more predictable splits — my father from my mother, my parents from me, each from ourselves. It is as if it was her skull that was the fragile chassis that cleaved in two.

As usual, my father turned away, his back more familiar to me than my own face. He retreated out the door, leaving me to my mother and her scissors. I let my mother snip a lock, it was just easier that way, and then she took ten instant Polaroid shots of my head from every conceivable angle, and one, inexplicably, of my feet.

My parents never tell stories about my childhood, our time in Jammu, the past, theirs or mine. They are a virtual tabula rasa, a brick wall, a bank vault sealed shut. Over the years, I have been a teacher with white chalk marking a lesson on the board, a renovator crafting a hole for a window in a windowless house, a thief cracking open a safe, combination unknown, with dynamite.

If my parents were to ever ask why I'm going, I would tell them I'm searching for my cousin Prithi, who I named my Barbie doll after, and my New Delhi aunt, who always made me my favourite breakfast dish — parathas with jam. I would tell them I'm searching for hope, the hope I've kept alive all these years, wrapped up in yellow cloth.

It's Madame Jaune that I've come all the way to India for. Madame Jaune, the nervy, never-married woman who always wore yellow saris. She worked as a botanist at my father's lab and invited us to elaborate dinners at her grand home. She showed us her riotous rose garden with modest pride, gave us a little kitten that mewled all night and had to be returned the next day, and just before we were to leave for Canada, placed her hand on my shoulder and asked my parents if she could adopt me.

I want to run into the folds of Madame Jaune's yellow sari, her bounteous lap and weep. I want to ask her what she saw in my family that made her want to adopt me. I want to ask her how she divined trouble, the nettle-paved road that was to be my future. I want to tell her now that I wished she had adopted me.

While my attention wandered, Prithi had neatly arranged the photos on the bed in chronological order. I see my three cousins, Prithi, Radha and Dinesh grow up in front of my eyes, skeletal youngsters with gap-toothed smiles morph into young men and women, rounded and solid with weight. In the last picture the three of them are lined up at the peeling painted metal gate of their courtyard, arms tight around one another, smiling and squinting into the sun. Prithi tells me, "Dinesh killed himself." I hear my Aunt Puspha cough and then sigh in the background. "He wanted to marry, but the girl's family objected to him because of caste," Prithi answers to my unspoken question. "He started to take drugs, heroin. He hung himself, here in the courtyard, when we were all asleep." Then, as if she can't stop herself, a boulder teetering on the edge of a cliff: "Radha was diagnosed with a brain tumour a year later. She died a few months after the operation." Prithi falls silent, while her words thud around me. She's gone back to being gauzy. The only living child of Makhan Chand and Puspha.

Makhan Chand shows me the flour mill he supervises to keep busy. It is a cavernous, round, stone building, and fine white flour seeps out of everywhere, the cracks in the masonry, even the burlap bags stacked high up against the wall. He sweeps his arm about the room, presenting to me his ledger, the clock on the wall, his calendar marking his schedules, his retirement watch that dangles on a gold chain. It is as if he means to orient me to the intimate spaces of his life, yet the space is empty of any mention of his two dead children. His gaze lingers, reluctant to part from each object he shows me. There's a sense of urgency in his voice, as if even these objects have a life and that life could be quickly snatched away.

"Makhan Chand Uncle," I suddenly say, my voice echoing in the big room. I have caught him in mid-sweep as he points to yet another object which he will present with the deepest of empathy. He turns to me with misty eyes, and I notice his eyes, like my aunt's, are blue-grey with cataracts.

"Do you remember a woman botanist who wore yellow saris, that we called 'Madame Jaune' as children?"

"Yes," he replies. He is puzzled by my question.

"Is she still alive?" I ask.

"Yes. She is retired." He pauses, scrolling his memory banks for something else to give me. "She still keeps a beautiful garden." Then he catches on to the reason behind my question. "Would you like to visit her? It could be arranged." He peers over his ledger, already rearranging his orderly schedule to accommodate me.

I hear his pocket watch ticking.

Makhan Chand fills the silence while I think. He resumes the presentation of his life. When again he shows the ledger, the walls of this space, his pocket watch to me, I can almost hear him saying, "Look, how hard the life of a watch is." I can hear the grief in his voice. I can see how he has made of his world a blank canvas on which he's poured all his grief. I can almost see his children, faint shadows, in the face of the Sherpa woman, in the walls of the flour mill, in the intimate workings of his pocket watch, keeping time for him. And like him, I, too, can almost see them everywhere.

Makhan Chand circles back to his question, rousing me from my reverie. "Would you like to visit her?" he asks me again.

But I am my father's daughter after all. "No," I say finally.

I think about Madame Jaune, the way she may look now, her head a shock of white, her hair thinning, knees arthritic, her lap, tender and fragile with age. I think of the way I am now, not a toddler, light as cotton, but a full-grown woman, heavy — heavy as the sacks of flour piled high in the corner. And I tell myself, surely I would break her bones if I hurled myself at her lap and wept.

❧ Honeymoon in Kashmir

Mandir knew his saris well and thought he knew women even better.

Not only could he identify the exact state and village a woman might have come from, a trait he shared with most Indians, but also he could predict precisely their preference in colour, patterns, materials and sari length. He knew which sari a customer might ask for and finger for a long time, and which one he would end up wrapping in brown butcher's paper. He knew a woman rarely chose what she truly desired, but what her family or husband's family thought appropriate.

When a mother on a buying spree chose her daughter's favourite colours and styles for her wedding dowry, he knew she was a beloved daughter. When a mother anticipated the husband-to-be or mother-in-law's taste, he knew how much the mother feared for her daughter's safety. He knew that when a woman's hands trembled back and forth over a fine *jamdani* muslin and then over an ordinary nylon, she was assessing how much damage to herself her choice might make and calculating if it was worth it for a brief moment of rebellion. With his mind's eye, he tried to move her hand to choose rebellion, for that was always more profitable for him.

He knew, too, which woman to refer to the tailor with the wandering hands who cut him a hefty percentage for the recommendation, and which woman would not stay silent, and thus hurt his potential easy profit.

Whether he was in a good mood or an angry one, he would make bets with his reluctant assistant, a distant and poor cousin his mother had insisted he take on.

"Sir, you have superior knowledge in this area. I am only in training," Rakesh begged not to be included in his game.

Despite his assistant's entreaties, Mandir would predict that the turquoise silk sari with the silver brocade border would find its way into the dowry chest of the young woman in the white embroidered *chouridhar* walking up the wooden steps with her mother. Or that the orange and green silk sari with *bandhani* work would be an ambitious present given to a high-priced whore by the bespectacled young university student with one shoulder pulled lower by his heavy cotton book bag.

Having announced his predictions, Mandir would thump Rakesh on his back, and Rakesh was forced to hastily put forward his own guess. Invariably, Mandir was right, winning his own bet and taking Rakesh's paltry earnings from him. With Rakesh's money he bought sweetmeats for his mother from Chand's Sweet Treats, the neighbouring stall. He stored the silver box of sweets under his counter, like his father before him, his ledger, dagger and *paan* laid out neatly, always ready for business, for trouble and for pleasure.

Mandir's Sari Emporium was one of forty shops lining the road in Ragunath, the commercial district of Jammu, a town most Indians ignored on the way to the Himalayas and their summer holidays in Kashmir. Once, a hippie from Manchester, England, had stopped by Mandir's stall to ask him for information. Mandir had served him chai in exchange for some news about the state of the British economy. The hippie wore his hair in a ponytail and carried a large mountaineering backpack. He had pointed to a page in a travel guide, "Not much to see," the book advised foreigners.

"Is this really true?" the hippie had asked, as if the people in Jammu were keeping a big secret from him.

"Forget Jammu. It's only Kashmir you want to visit. Number one honeymoon vacation site," Mandir replied. "You have not seen our Hindi films? Everyone singing, also dancing, in the mountains. Like your *Sound of Music*. Go there, you'll see."

Now foreigners rarely visited, only reporters on their way to Kashmir, where trouble lay waiting on the ledges and in the crags of the mountains, even at the highest altitudes.

Traffic was local, three-wheel taxis, rickshaws, or people on foot, their *chappals* slapping the paved road. On a busy day, which was most days, a car could not get past the throng of shoppers busy in the street. The stores were mostly wooden cubes joined together and elevated a few feet above the ground as a protection against floods. To get into a unit, one had to climb a few steps. Each unit was not more than two rooms deep; the front part where the wares were displayed, and the back part where goods were stored and certain business transacted away from prying eyes.

Mandir had only been a boy in short pants, his school satchel already too heavy for him, marking the starched white shirt of his school uniform, when he had been expected to begin serving his father, to learn from him, and then to inherit the store when his father died. His father, Ramesh, had been the only son born in a run of five daughters. His grandfather, who owned several shops in the area, had chosen to divest all but one of his businesses, rather than try and find suitable men who could marry his daughters and run his profitable enterprises.

"I would rather sell my businesses than see them destroyed by a stupid son-in-law," his grandfather had told the matchmaker his grandmother had invited for chai, sweets and her famous pakoras.

Mandir's father, Ramesh, was just a boy at the time, and very attached to his sisters. He did not want to see his sisters, who had included him in their games and taught him how to chew *paan* and to play cricket, married off, to only return, if at all, for short visits determined by a persnickety mother-in-law.

"Surely, my father could have found one man in all of India who could have run his business and not destroyed it," Mandir heard his father say to company, his words laced with bitterness. His father often walked by the stores that had been sold, pulling Mandir along to stare, an unrequited lover, bitter at the way they had been sullied by others' hands. Holding his father's hand, Mandir thought he could hear his father's heart pumping and beating, like a drum in the old days, calling for help.

Sometimes, if Mandir was feeling indulgent and if he liked a woman's look, say the shape of her eyebrows, natural, not plucked with a high arch, or the colour of her skin, fair and flawless, he might lay before such a woman what she secretly hungered for, but would or could never buy. He took pleasure in the way her hands caressed a garden silk or the way her fingers read the filigree on his wedding saris, the *zari*, a heavily brocaded silk sari from the best weavers in Benares.

But what Mandir waited for, with the utmost patience, was the way a woman might, in losing herself in the exquisite specimen he had selected for her and had known she would covet, forget herself and her chaperones (for no woman ever came without accompaniment to his store). He waited for the moment he knew would come, knowing her well, when she put the cloth to her cheek as if it were the face of a lover. And when she draped the *pallou* end of a sari over her head and across her chest, stroking her breasts in the process, he held his breath, closed his eyes and tried to memorize the movement of her hands over her body and his silk. Then the disapproving voice of the mother-in-law, or sometimes an older sister-in-law, would corrode the edges of his fledgling fantasy.

"What use have you for such a sari? We are not coming for a ball gown. *Bhai*, bring me the nylon one. So much more practical, nuh?"

It was at moments like these that Mandir hated the social restrictions on women. When sufficiently drunk on toddy in the town's only den of vice, a wooden liquor stall hidden in the warren of alleys behind the stores, Mandir would sometimes try and instigate a discussion on the status of women in India.

"The problems of women are my problems," he would say, pounding his fist on his chest.

Some Marxist, new to the town, and equally drunk on the dark drink, might slosh his glass around and give a toast to the businessman, a bourgeois who supported women's emancipation. And so encouraged, Mandir would continue expounding his views.

"If women were freer, I would be a happier man." To which the Marxist would reply, "Hear, hear!"

But the rest of the stall patrons would snicker, and a string of dirty jokes, the majority of which featured Mandir in several undignified positions, would drown out even the loudest scooters, three-wheel taxis and tourist buses belching through the back alley where the liquor stall served its customers.

Undeterred, Mandir continued. "If women could choose their hearts' desire, could pick their own saris from a pile of the best in my shop, I would be a richer man. What woman would ever pick a nylon sari for herself if she had the freedom to choose and money in her own pocket? It would all be silk!"

Here the Marxist would snort in derision, not at Mandir, but at his own folly to even have thought a businessman could ever put aside material greed. And Mandir, having lost his prompter, would sink into quietude, mulling over his last memory of a woman holding a modest Japanese silk to her breast, until Balbir, his mother's servant, came to fetch him home.

The wooden stores carried sound easily through their slats. Mandir had developed a habit of listening to BBC on the radio and to Amina, the daughter of Satish Chand in the sweet shop next to his. He liked her voice, the way her excited words spilled over themselves like water bubbling over rocks in a fast-moving stream.

When her school chums, a serious and studious lot, came to visit, they sat on the floor, a little out of the way of customers, completing their math homework, their stick legs in fashionable *chouridhars*, dangling over the edge. Mandir could see them from where he stood behind his cash register, his fingers lightly tapping the keys, bored. The wooden cubes shared a common walkway, a lip, where shoppers could go from store to store without climbing up and down the stairs that led them to the street. When the girls had finished, they would sip Thumbs Up or Fanta Orange with straws, their brows furrowed, and watch the procession of shoppers packing the street. Sometimes they would hold hands in companionable silence.

It was a paradox that well-loved children were well-loved by the world, but unloved children were usually badly treated. In Amina's case, customers would buy an extra *ladoo* or *jalebi* to offer to the girl, despite the obvious fact that her father doted on her.

"Such a good girl. I wish my Baloo would study so hard," they would say, pinching her cheek.

And Amina, refusing the sweet politely, would reply over and over again, "Thank you, Uncle-ji, thank you Auntie-ji, but Papa gives me everything I want."

When all the children, except of course the servant children, were at school, Satish would visit with Mandir, offering samosas. They would roll some *paan* together and sit at the edge of the stall, spitting the red liquid into the open drain that ran the length of the road.

"Trouble in the house again," Satish would begin. "My wife wishes for Amina to go to college and get her BSc but my own mother wishes otherwise. How can I keep peace in the house? What is the correct thing to do?"

He would wait for Mandir to reply. But Mandir had learned from his father two things: one, the way to invite confidences was to stay silent and, two, that people often confused silence with wisdom. Mandir wanted Satish's vote to re-elect him to the Merchants' Association on which he sat as president of their district, so Mandir stayed silent. The truth was that Mandir was just as confused as Satish; his fondness for the girl led him to want to indulge her as her father did, but in general, he was of the opinion that girls should not bother going on to college if they were to be married.

Satish continued, "I am just an uneducated man. If Indira Gandhi is wishing for girls to continue their studies, who am I to criticize the Prime Minister?" Satish would cock his head, like a rooster surprised by his own voice, his question answered. Relieved, he would then go for his morning constitutional, a little walk up and down the street, while keeping a practiced eye on the stall and its register for pilferers.

It had been many years since Amina sat on the floor of her father's stall. She had been busy with college and, except for a few fleeting sightings, it was the first time Mandir saw her again at her father's shop. She was in a printed cotton sari bought from a rival sari shop, a shade of pink a little too bright for her medium complexion, a colour he was certain he would never have advised her to wear.

Amina was shouting. "I don't want to get married. I want to run this business and make it prosper. It's all I've ever wanted. How could you conspire behind my back and try to arrange a marriage? I will not agree to it. I tell you now, I will not!"

He did not hear her father's reply, only saw Amina flounce out, her *pallou* billowing out behind her, her long plait a whip snapping to the beat of her *chappals*.

A year or two passed. Amina suddenly appeared behind the counter at Chand's Sweet Shop. Her father was bedridden, serious heart trouble, Amina told Mandir. She would be running the shop now. Mandir took to visiting her shop; she never came to his, perhaps afraid of what people might say. He bought sweets, more than he normally bought, and hovered around the glass case, hoping she would indulge him in a bit of conversation. She was always civil, though curt, never meeting his eyes, instead wiping the glass counter or rearranging the *ladoos* with a pair of silver tongs.

"What is the news on the Merchants' Association?" she asked, after many weeks of rote conversation. "My father wants to know," she added, as if he might not tell her otherwise.

"Of course." Mandir managed to stutter the news: the recent motion to widen the streets, the successful resolution between two shopkeepers about a refuse pile behind their shop, the ratification of a bylaw to increase the Association's dues collection. And, as she listened attentively, he thought he spied an opening, the tiniest of rents in six yards of cloth that the fussiest of his customers would never have noticed. He went through it headfirst, like a father he once saw diving into a well to rescue his drowning toddler, diving without forethought, without hesitation. At the bottom of the well, reflected in the water, he saw moving pictures — Amina running around a tree in the lushness of Kashmir, her eyes heavily kohl-rimmed, her *pallou* falling off her shoulder, revealing smooth skin, and he, a younger version of himself, in a dashing *khadi kameez* chasing after her. His visions shocked him, but a surge of excitement flitted through his body.

He was lonely. And he was tired of visiting the whore who called herself Lakshmi who he had been frequenting for years, a woman who laughed at him when he proffered yet again another expensive sari. Though he chose the sari with care and to complement her beauty, he chose it from the pile he marked for giveaways, saris with slight defects that most women were sharp enough to pick out, spreading the whole length on his counter for examination just before buying. Somehow, Mandir had thought Lakshmi wouldn't notice, or maybe if she noticed, wouldn't care, grateful for the symbol of his interest in her. But lately, since Amina had come to work, two things had started to bother him — Lakshmi's laughter, and that, invariably, Lakshmi's female servant, not the whore, would wear the sari he had given Lakshmi on his last visit.

Mandir noticed that Amina had been making many changes to the store. There was a wooden chair in a corner, that she had placed for pregnant women and the elderly so that they could rest while awaiting their orders. She had disposed of the statue of Ganesh, and replaced the Hindu calendar that always hung on the back wall with a calendar of the natural wonders of the world. She said her uncle in Canada had given it to her on his only visit back to Jammu. It was ten years out of date. Today, it was open to the Grand Canyon, a picture of brilliant oranges and red and black shadows. She had kept the garlanded pictures of her grandfather and great-grandfather that always adorned the wall on a narrow shelf, but she had added one of her mother, one of her aunts and one of her grandmother. Plump red roses and marigolds also festooned the shelf. Brilliant Rajasthani mirror work cloths snuggled against the shop's side walls. The wooden floor had been resurfaced with indigo paint and polished with wax. Beside the cash register, Mandir noticed with distaste, was a collection jar asking for donations to fund the formation of women's handicraft and sewing co-operatives.

Once, Mandir had stood patiently to the side, waiting to get Amina's attention. Unlike her father, Amina served people in the order of their arrival, only making exceptions for obviously pregnant women and the sick or old. She did not, as most shopkeepers did, make Dalits wait even if they had arrived first, or serve a rich person before a poorer one. Unlike most stores, where chaos reigned and, on busy days, men and women jostled each other meanly, her customers stood in a respectful line. She changed the shop's name to India's Best Little Sweet Shop. What customers she lost to the more clearly identifiable Hindu-owned shop a few stores down, she gained in Muslim and Dalit clients. If the men, mostly Hindu fundamentalists, huffed and puffed at the back of the line, muttering under their breaths at the new order of things, women, for the most part, admired her fairness and stood politely in line and smiled at each other. They knew, by the weight of the rupees still left rolled up in their sari blouse or tied up in a knot at the end of their *pallou*, that she had not cheated them as her father had.

Mandir had also watched the Marxist he'd once had drinks with walk into Amina's store with a sheaf of flyers. The man had lingered for a long time as Amina served customers. Mandir could hear the cash register pinging furiously. During a lull, hearing no voices next door, Mandir had walked over to her store, curious. He had found them in the back room, the Marxist gesticulating widely, but whispering softly.

"… and this practice of using human shields has been reported many, many times. Women and children have gone missing, too. The soldiers are raping with impunity. Massacres by the Indian Army have been well documented …" Amina had abruptly hidden the flyers under a stack of the silver carton boxes when she saw Mandir walk in.

Mandir had waited till the Marxist left.

"*Beti*, in business, appearances are everything. You might think, what harm can there be looking at his flyers? But be aware that army informants are everywhere. The army has suffered many casualties in Kashmir, and they may harass you, even kill you, on the mere suspicion that you are a sympathizer. And the Kashmiri extremists, they may come to you thinking you *are* a sympathizer and before you know it they are making you do things you don't want to do."

"But Uncle-ji …" Amina stood ready to argue, the tilt of her head defiant. It was the first time Amina had looked at him directly, her eyes meeting his own. The connection Mandir felt was electric. Mandir's knees gave away, and he fell into the painted wooden chair Amina reserved for her pregnant customers. Amina reached to steady him, a reflexive move, but then she jerked her hand back before it could make contact.

"No, no, no need for explanations. I know you are a young girl and you didn't mean anything by it. Give me the flyers and I will see that they are destroyed." She handed him the flyers and Mandir, now aware that he had potentially incendiary material in his own hands, became nervous. "Quick, give me a bag." He stood and stuffed the flyers in the bag, looked nervously into the street, and then walked over to his stall. He called Rakesh into the back room, handing over the flyers to him. "Burn these. Immediately." And having done his duty, he slapped his hands against his trousers, as if wiping them clean before heading over to the front counter for a bit of toddy and *paan* to calm his heart beating as fast as a riff by a tabla player in a frenzy.

Then one quiet day, Mandir overheard Amina speaking to a customer.

"The tailor in Gandhinagar is not for you, Madam. He has a reputation for cheating and of being disrespectful to women and girls," Amina said.

Without thinking, he marched around the corner, incensed. How dare she malign his tailor! How dare she cut into his profits! It was those profits that helped him buy the latest appliances for his mother: an electric water warmer, a new radio, a satellite dish for the television. No one had ever accused the tailor of impropriety. What right had she then to spread harmful tales?

At the counter, a woman in her twenties stood smiling at Amina. Mandir had just served her, she had bought three yards of pale pink cotton. She was new to Jammu, still wearing a sari in the bright colours of the south, emerald green, saffron, and pink. She said her husband, an orthopedic doctor, had been stationed here to work in the army hospital and she wanted some new clothes so that she would not stand out so much. She had never worn a *salwar kameez* before, maybe she would have one or two made for herself.

Amina smiled back at the woman. "The sewing co-operative is better. Only women. You will encounter no problems. And your business will benefit widows and poor women." She handed the woman from the south a flyer.

When Amina saw Mandir hovering at the stall's edge, she smiled, a smile like the one Lakshmi gave him sometimes when she saw him appear at her gate, a mango in one hand, a brown paper–wrapped sari in the other. An unfathomable smile.

Mandir started to speak, but choked on his words, pretending he had a cough. There would be another way, he thought, wiping his forehead with his handkerchief. He could not just charge in here like a braying donkey. Perhaps he should visit Satish soon. After all, Satish was still her father and the owner of the store. Mandir would ask him what he thought of all the changes Amina was making to his store, his father's store, his father's father's store.

But just before the monsoons came, when the sky was a thirsty beast sucking the rivers and reservoirs dry, and water and electricity curfews were imposed, Amina came to him. Her generator could not keep up with running both the cooler and her electric fans, and perhaps, too, it was running a bit more inefficiently after the last dust storm, a particularly ferocious storm that Mandir well remembered. Rakesh was still, a week later, sweeping his shop floor of sand and wiping surfaces free of grit.

"I am afraid the milk will not keep. I will have to throw out kilos of *ras malai* and the poor woman who makes them for me will suffer. I would ask my father what to do, but he's not well."

Mandir immediately offered to help. He sent Rakesh to look at her generator and when the boy had not come back by the time he had served twenty customers already, he cursed, pulling the rolling metal door down from the roof and locking the stall.

Rakesh was sitting on several tins of condensed milk, sipping chai, looking at Amina. Amina was leaning against the wall, staring out the open back door. The Himalayas were craggy humps, blue in the distance. The room was still except for the chugging generator shaking like a feverish malaria patient outside.

Mandir knew he had made a mistake. He had never truly looked at Rakesh before. Had never seen the dimples in his cheeks, the cleft in his chin, the long eyelashes that shadowed his cheeks. In his mind, Rakesh was still the thin, barefoot boy chasing a bicycle tire with a stick along the goat path that he had met a long time ago on a family visit to Poonch. Mandir noted, with distress, that Rakesh had filled out since then and his long limbs were awkwardly bent in the small back room. Mandir wanted to upend the delicate teacup balanced precariously on Rakesh's knee, to kick his feet out from beneath him.

He wanted to shout at Rakesh, *Bloody fool, who do you think you are, a Maharaja, a British Governor maybe? Sitting here sipping tea as if you are a king and not a servant!* Mandir had to think, to not let emotion rule. To berate Rakesh in front of Amina, who was too good-hearted for her own good, might serve to lessen him in her eyes. He had started to understand that Amina loved the weak and powerless. A man such as himself, a man of power, would have to be very careful if he wanted to win her over.

"I see your generator is fixed," he said to Amina, and forced himself to smile jovially when she jerked, startled. Rakesh, he noticed with some satisfaction, leapt to his feet, the tea sloshing over the rim of the saucer.

"Thank you. You have been very kind. Please, please take as many sweets as you would like to your mother," Amina said, brushing past him into the store front, sliding open the cooler's window and grabbing the tongs. Normally, he would have given her a wide berth, would have cast his eyes down as a sign of respect, but he wasn't feeling generous today. He had felt her as she brushed by, the naked part of her arm where her *dupatta* did not cover had touched his skin, like a naan freshly baked, warm but cooling, soft and dusty. It made him want to touch her again.

"I have been thinking of visiting your father since he is not so well." Mandir positioned himself behind her, a few inches too close. He could feel her back stiffen. "May I visit him tomorrow?"

"Of course," Amina replied, steady in her speech, but he saw that the presentation of sweets in their silver carton box, usually neat, was untidy, one *ladoo* broken in half, crushed by the others jammed up too tight against it. He thought he had heard the tinge of guilt in her response, but he still did not feel satisfied.

At Satish's house, in the front parlor, his wife served Mandir pakoras and chai, making polite conversation before escorting him to the spartan bedroom.

"What does the doctor say?" Mandir asked the gaunt man in the bed whom he barely recognized as Satish. Satish had lost several kilos, his eyes were dark troughs, his chest had sunk so much his collar bones looked liked they had erupted from beneath his skin to sit on the outside of his chest. Though Mandir asked the question, he already knew the answer from Balbir, his mother's servant. It was incurable. Satish would not live to serve sweets at the festival of Holi again.

"Bah, these modern doctors, they won't even touch you. What can they know?" Satish coughed and dabbed at his nose with a handkerchief. "I'm going to live for a long time. Long enough to drink another drink with my good friend." Satish laughed, pointing to the lemonade jug on a small table underneath the window. On the windowsill, tiny brown bottles with shiny silver tops were lined up like soldiers. There were syringes, too, and cotton wool in a tiny tin cup.

Mandir joined Satish in laughter and poured a glass of lemonade for him. "Satish, my friend, you are a good businessman, maybe even a great businessman, and you and I, we know that in life just as in business, it is good to always be prepared for any outcome, no?"

"Not to worry. I have made all the necessary preparations, my friend. My only concern is that my daughter be married well, but I will live to see her wedding." Satish raised his glass in toast, as if he was already at her wedding feast.

"I have always been fond of your daughter," Mandir said, surprised by the sudden trembling of his voice and the cold sweat stunning his armpits. "I have been watching her progress in your store. She has done well for herself."

"Oh, my daughter, she is a very smart girl. Very smart girl," Satish replied, his voice trembling with pride. As if searching for her, his eyes drifted to the rooms beyond his own, tearing with the effort.

Mandir jumped into the soliloquy he had rehearsed that morning as he shaved in front of the mirror. "But the others are talking. Some of the changes she has made are creating controversy. May even lead to danger. I am afraid for her, and for you."

"What changes? What changes?" Satish sat up abruptly, causing a frightening round of coughing.

So it was as Mandir thought, Amina had not consulted her father about these changes. It was then an easy matter to fill Satish in, while sipping lemonade. It was easy to spell out the implications, and then to sit back and watch Satish struggle with the decision he knew he would have to make.

And when Satish finally reached the right decision, his wife interrupting their haggling with her incessant fussing, it was very late at night. Walking home exhilarated by the exchange, the roosters about to start their crowing, Mandir planned his wedding — which one of his best wedding *zaris* to set aside for Amina, what silk to use for his wedding pajamas, which guests to invite.

Even though he knew Amina had not yet agreed to the marriage, he could not contain his excitement. He even allowed his mother to consult with the astrologer for an auspicious day for the marriage. When the bent old man came to the house bearing his scrolls, Mandir, on impulse, asked him for a review of his own astrological chart to see what other happiness lay in store for him. The astrologer assured him that he would be a rich man (which was already true), that he would live a long life, and that he would find himself in the arms of a woman he had wanted for a long time. He was warned to stay away from toddy, because he would have liver problems if he did not, and he was warned to be kind to others, for if he was not, they would, like a pet scorpion, bite him back one day.

So Mandir instructed his mother to give alms to the beggars that came to their door. He visited the local orphanage and gave a thick stack of rupees to the Grey Nuns. He resolved that, on his wedding day, he would feed all the poor who came to sit outside and watch, no matter how the news spread and how many mouths to feed that meant. He even went to his mother's temple and did a puja for his father and his father before him.

In short, Mandir was happy, deliriously happy. The ink on the sale of the business, Satish's store, was dry, the old notary had completed all the paperwork. "Lucky man, two stores now. Your father would be proud of you," the notary said to him, collecting his papers and slipping them into a leather satchel. Mandir felt tears of happiness come to his eyes. He wiped them surreptitiously, thumped the old man on the back, and invited him to the wedding. "To be married, too? Ah, you are a twice lucky man!" the notary had chortled.

But as the days passed, there were no messengers from Satish's house bearing the good news of Amina's acceptance. The money Mandir had paid to Satish to buy his sweet shop would come back to him at the marriage as a dowry from Satish. He didn't understand what was causing the delay.

At their morning tea, his mother urged him not to pressure Satish. Mandir had thrust his morning paper aside in frustration, unable to read, unable to sip his tea without spilling it. He felt tortured. He might as well listen to his mother; perhaps she could provide insight into his troubles. "Understandably, the girl will have to get used to the idea. After all, you are almost as old as her father." Mandir had never thought of himself as an unsuitable match for Amina before. After all, wasn't he a wealthy and respected businessman?

His mother raised herself out of the teak chair with difficulty, her bones creaking, her silk sari rustling, her gold earrings tinkling, to stand beside him. She patted him absent-mindedly on the shoulder while thinking out loud, "And her father is not well. She may feel she is not ready to leave the family at this time. Give her time. She is a good girl. She will do as her father wishes."

Somehow, Mandir did not feel comforted. The idea of Amina coming to him only because her father wished it troubled him. He wanted her to desire the idea of him, to desire him. He felt again as if he was plunging headlong into a well, and there were no comforting pictures of Amina running around a tree in Kashmir to bedazzle him. Instead, when he closed his eyes to try and think, he saw an emaciated Amina, drugged and bedraggled, on the wedding platform, shrouded in the heaviest of threaded gold saris. And when he lifted the veil, he saw Satish's face, a skull, smiling perpetually as skulls do.

As all bad news comes, it came first by way of the servant's grapevine. Amina, Balbir told him, had run away to New Delhi to work in an NGO that helped establish women's co-operatives in the Kutch desert. She had found this post through the Marxist who sometimes visited her store, and though many suspected a romantic involvement, the mother was sure that this was not the case. The Marxist was still in Jammu and her daughter was clearly not pregnant for she had checked her rags for blood herself.

Though her mother had initially agreed with her husband that Amina should be disowned, at the last minute she had changed her mind, dashing through the streets to the train station, rupees stuffed in her brassiere and in a bag. The servants had found one of the courtyard stones upturned, a hole in the ground where a metal money box lay open but devoid of its rupees. Her mother had found Amina at the train station alone and weeping into her *dupatta*. She had kissed her daughter, handed her the bag of money and put her on the rust-coloured train, urging her to write and call. Then she had turned away and walked all the way home alone to face her dying husband.

When the bomb exploded on their street, ripping apart Amina's (now his) padlocked store, the store next door, and the front half of his own sari shop, Mandir was visiting Lakshmi. He was drowning his sorrows in her arms and in toddy, berating himself for his miscalculation, for being a frog in a well, knowing only the deep, dark dankness of his stone enclosure.

"Lovers dancing in the hills of Kashmir? Bah! Kashmir is a bloody war zone! These stupid lovers are prancing in fields of land mines!" Mandir was just lifting his heavy head from Lakshmi's warm bosom to continue his tirade against the Hindi film industry, when Lakshmi's servant, wearing the sari Mandir had given Lakshmi on his last visit, sidled into their room to point at the window where Rakesh paced at the courtyard gate. Rakesh called him out into the courtyard to deliver the news of the bombing, too embarrassed to set foot in a house of ill repute.

That night, the army would come, as they always did, by the truckful and trainload. They would impose a curfew, slamming anyone, Hindus, Muslims, Sikhs, Dalits, on their heads with the butt of their rifles if they dared to be caught after curfew. Their victims would lie on the street spread-eagled, stunned, ears bloodied, a ring of grey-helmeted soldiers pointing guns at every part of their body.

Before the army arrived, Mandir raced over to his dismembered store, taking in the sight of planks of wood hanging like peeling skin, his one mannequin, once shrouded by the most exquisite red filigree *zari*, now engulfed in flames like a tested Sita or a victim of dowry burning. Next door, glass shards from the cooler littered the caved-in floor, and the steps to the shop he had once climbed with such hope lay separated from the store, like an amputated leg. He had lost two stores. He had lost Amina. His life was ruined.

Mandir fell to the ground, oblivious to the pain in his knees as glass pierced his flesh. He realized with sudden horror that if he had not been so lovelorn and distraught, he would not have closed the store early to visit Lakshmi. Instead, he would have been ping-pinging at the keys of his new electronic cash register, watching wealth flow into its cupped drawers before the bomb ripped apart his limbs. And he realized with even greater horror that if he had not made his deal with Satish, the store next door, Amina's store, would not have been closed. Amina would have been there, his Amina, serving her Dalits, her Marxists, her pregnant women, handing out flyers. She would have been blown away into the night sky. Her life would have faded, like the mountains fading into blue in the distance.

And then, it occurred to him, and the realization seized his heart, a sudden cramping as if he had just jumped into the glacial water of the Himalayas, excruciatingly painful, but refreshing: yes, he lay in the ruin of his life, yes, life had, in the most mysterious and per-verted way, played its biggest cosmological joke on him — yes, he had indeed lost Amina, but he *had* saved her life.

❧ THE BOY HE LEFT BEHIND

I HAD BEEN DODGING THE BACKWARD GLANCE ALL MY LIFE. IT'S
something my father taught me when he bought me, his only son, a
one-way ticket to Canada meaning for me to never return. But then
my mother died and all I could do was lie in bed in a funk staring
at the stippled white ceiling as if it were a screen and my bedroom
an empty cinema playing the story of my sorry life. My dreams, and
nightmares too, were suffused with Technicolor images of my mother
and of Hussain, a delicate boy I had known briefly in childhood, who
had later gone missing.

Marcel, my sometime lover, finally roused me from my rum-in-
duced haze. "Go and deal with your demons," he said, fed up. He
tossed some letters on my chest, blue envelopes with violet markings
and the stamp of India. They were from my distant relatives in
Kashmir wondering what to do with my mother's ashes, begging for
my return and offering a nice sum for the family estate — a house and
five hundred acres of rice fields. It occurred to me that while I was
there, perhaps, just perhaps, I could try to find Hussain. The thought
revived me, but I didn't tell Marcel about Hussain. Hussain was an airy
dream, ethereal. I could pass my hand through him, like a cone of light
from a film projector.

Marcel kissed me at the check-in counter in full view of the service
representative weighing my luggage. The service rep was a crisp Girl
Guide in blue serge and a requisite silk scarf noosed around her neck,
but she looked away shyly and twiddled with the tags on my bags to
give us more time. Still, I was uncomfortable and prematurely ejected

from the kiss. No doubt it would have been a long and passionate one with a good deal of tongue twirling and tongue sucking, causing twitters to ripple through the long line of people inching towards their eventual destinations. I couldn't tell if the kiss would be our last one. I was a chemist and made adhesive formulas for my clients, but I had never quite figured out a formula to make love stick. Yes, I stuck to Marcel and he to me, but like a Post-it Note that had lost its tackiness and was constantly falling off the refrigerator. My mood swings, made wilder by a penchant for the St. Lucian rum that Marcel had introduced me to, hadn't helped. Before Marcel, it had been orange juice and vodka and white men. Marcel joked that I should be on lithium. I was high-strung, and often giddy, it was true, but I blamed the ether I was forced to inhale at the lab. When I was thousands of miles away, would Marcel come to his senses, finally leave me for a handsome political science professor? Another graduate student? Some guy, well-muscled with degrees, he met at the university gym?

My driver navigated the rutted roads up to my mother's village. I had nothing to do but stare out the bug-splattered window and think of her. Large expanses of field flew by: the farms of Kashmir, frowzy-haired wheat sunning in the wind, rice paddies in their shallow rippling ponds, short shrubs shimmying for the best light. Soil rich in yield, begetting cabbages so heavy and round they were sometimes referred to as expectant, like pregnant women.

I ran through those fields once, on my way to Hussain before he disappeared, my red silk kite a gift from my mother on my fifteenth birthday, its yellow trailers streaming behind me high in the air. The day had been fat, like a well-fed boy in a too-tight vest, and I had been satiated on the rosewater sweetness of *ras gullas* and electrified by the harmonic convergence of the universe that had moved my normally undemonstrative parents to fashion a birthday for me complete with sparklers and gifts. As I ran to show off my kite to Hussain, my feet squelching in the mud of the *brinjal* patch, I knew my parents were sitting on the verandah watching me, their eyes glinting with pride. I have never again been so happy as in that moment.

When I first booked my flight, I was sure I wouldn't stay at my mother's house. I wanted boiled water, toilet paper and hot showers, not cold water bucket baths. I had changed that much. I had even registered at the five-star hotel in Srinagar, fifty kilometres away, but when I arrived at my mother's house, the long line of people, the vigilant hospitality of my mother's relatives, the servants' affronted looks when I mentioned the Rajput, had made it impossible for me to keep the room. In the end, I had to send my driver back to the hotel to retrieve my suitcases, those hard shells clamped tightly around the signifiers of my life abroad; the ready-made perma-press shirts, close-toed shoes, electric shaver with voltage adaptor, and a cornucopia of toiletries for every possible skin condition.

I felt dislocated, lost somehow, as if I had never arrived in my mother's village but was still somewhere on a long road that looped crazily back upon itself. Yet, bleary-eyed with exhaustion, I fulfilled my obligations as my mother's only son. My tongue, stiffened by English, finally loosened with the all-night card games my cousins insisted upon and the homemade toddy they plied me with, and my hearing finally readjusted its dial to the station of my mother tongue. I wore my old *khadi kurta,* reeking of mothballs but soft as silk, that the servant had pulled out of a well-polished tin trunk, and felt less myself and more myself. A relative lent me his *chappals* so my toes could breathe in the balmy air. Finally, I closed the sale with Jai, my mother's second cousin's son, and made a small fortune in Indian terms. I was a good feudal lord, did my duty and paid the loyal servants and field hands a hefty pension as my mother had instructed me in her last letter.

Jai, with his wife, Neelum, would raise his young children as my parents had, among the rows of vegetables and lakes of rice paddies, cradled in the lap of the Himalayas. I was free to leave India again, free to return to Marcel, but something pulled at me. I thought, perhaps, it was my mother, the way she had returned to me when I first stepped across the threshold of the house, her ashes in an urn on the walnut table waiting for me. I had a sense she had not finished with me.

Jai had the body of rural men all over India: thin and wiry from heavy chores on the family farm, the endless kilometres of walking to the nearest bus stop, the cyclical bouts of typhoid fever and of malaria. Nevertheless, he was impossibly handsome, baby-faced, with cheekbones in flight. And though we perched together on the string cot in the courtyard, smoking *bidis* in a comfortable silence, staring at the setting sun shielding its gold riches from covetous eyes of day, I resented his presence, resented him from the moment he had signed his name, with a wavering hand no less, to the legal papers that assigned him my mother's house.

"You never married?" Jai asked, while his son and daughter ran about the courtyard, arms extended, roaring like airplanes. *Father, look, we're flying! We're going abroad! Say goodbye! Say goodbye!*

I had anticipated this question, and I had rehearsed my answer a hundred times while sitting in the tiny egg cup that passed for a plane seat and downing many tiny bottles of tequila. I tossed him my cryptic "Life is different in the West," but Jai ignored the slight. Instead, he waved goodbye to his children buzzing down the runways of the vegetable garden before speaking again.

"What will you do with her ashes?" Jai changed the subject, sensing my discomfort.

"She wrote to me before she died. Not the Ganga. Too polluted. The river behind the house should please her."

"All rivers are like the Ganga," he said.

"She wanted to remain here." I felt the need to defend her wishes.

"She very much liked her pomegranate trees," Jai nodded, and his sensitivity made me dislike him even more.

Jai had spent the last year with my mother, his wife taking care of her, turning her in the bed, feeding her *kheer*, changing her soiled sheets, while Jai managed the farm. I would never forgive him for it. I had not even returned to light my father's or mother's funeral pyre, like an only son should. Jai had stood in for me, made easy excuses for me. "Canada is so far away. Your work is very important. Not so easy to leave."

A sudden urge for liquid anesthetic and body contact in dark and enclosed spaces overtook me. I could do with the azalea bushes behind the greenhouse at Allan Gardens, the pulsating gravel roof of a factory-turned-dance bar, or even the guano-encrusted pier at Kew Beach. I could taste vodka and dust and forgetting on my lips, and it made me reckless. I pointed to the neighbouring farm and finally asked my question. "What do you know of the boy who used to live a few kilometres that way?"

"Rashid's boy? Hussain?"

I nodded.

Jai looked at me, one eyebrow cocked in question. "His mother still lives there. She often visited your mother. But I don't know about Hussain. I was busy with the farm."

"Would your wife know?"

Jai walked into the house to consult with Neelum, a tall plump woman with wind-stung red cheeks. I could see them through the open door, framed in the kitchen, but their voices were too low for me to hear. Neelum was pumping the propane stove to prime it, getting ready to make our dinner.

Jai reappeared and sat down beside me again. "She says it is a confusing story. You must ask her yourself." His hand twisted his watch strap around his bony wrist so that its heavy face looked down towards the dusty floor of the compound.

I recognized my father's watch, its worn leather strap, scratched glass, the numbers in Hindi script. I had last seen it on my father's wrist twenty-five years ago. Memories, like jump cuts, ambushed me. Preparing for my exams at the town's sprawling red-brick school-house with the muddy cricket field. My father patting me on my shoulder when the list of marks posted on the wall by the school gate revealed mine to be the highest. His watch, always loose on his wrist, bouncing with his excitement.

"My son, you will surely go abroad with these marks. A scholarship is in sight for you." My father was a tall but stooped man, made sickly by a persistent cough that pulled his spine out of alignment, changing the shape of his rib cage. But that day, it seemed he walked upright, his hopes stronger than gravity, stronger than the pull of his illness.

Hussain was behind my father's eagerness to see me go abroad. That day of my birthday, my father had stumbled through the darkness of our storeroom on an errand for my mother and found us instead. We were reclining on a small hill of burlap bags, bags containing our winter provision of rice, lentils and mung beans. Our shorts were unbuttoned, and we were holding, not for the first time, each other's penis in our hands. My birthday kite, poised and ready for flight, lay next to me. Hussain managed to scrabble past him, but my father caught me and yanked me out of the storeroom, that room of pleasure and possibilities, by my ears. The daylight was urine-coloured and stung my eyes. "But my kite!" I had pleaded, not knowing what else to say.

My father had shouted, "Where did you learn such things?" He had forgotten the love showered on me earlier and had no regard for the asylum from discipline that my birthdays usually afforded me. Cuffs to my head and sharp kicks to my bottom followed. I was thrown unceremoniously onto the cot in my bedroom and the door bolted. My father had never hit me before. I had been mortified. "You will stay away from that crazy boy, that crazy man's son!" he thundered at me. I was glad for the thickness of the walnut door between us. The filter that weakened this, his new voice. I was to never play with Hussain again, never to speak to him, never to even look at him.

At school the next day I could see that Hussain had been caned by his father too, Hussain's legs striped with red welts, his face bruised yellow-purple and swollen. Had my father told Hussain's father about what he had seen, or had a field hand overheard my father's angry shouts and delivered the news? The other boys gingerly patted his back in a wordless show of sympathy, but when Hussain approached me in the courtyard, his eyes moist, his chin trembling, I turned away, scared that somehow word might reach my father if we spoke.

Jai coughed, interrupting my thoughts. My *bidi* had eroded to the tip, and the burning leaves were singeing my fingertips.

"A mother's love," he said, "makes many excuses."

Was he referring to Hussain? Or perhaps he was referring to Hussain's father, his reputation for violence; belts, shoes and canes, not just aimed at his son, but also his wife, the servants, even the occasional friend. Jai lit another *bidi* for me and we continued to puff out white curlicues of thought that hovered between us like a screen. Something overtook me, a desire to rip through the lace of our unspoken conversation, to ravage truth. I thought about seating Marcel on the cot between us, saying his name aloud, revealing his role in my life. What did I have to lose? Either people loved you or they didn't.

My father seemed to roll what he had seen in the storeroom into a tiny ball, like a scrap of paper, small and easy to lose in a deep pocket. Within weeks our relationship seemed to return to normal save for his ferocious quest to better my marks. My father drilled me in my subjects till the kerosene lanterns had to be refilled, night after night. Relentless, as if both our lives depended on perfect scores.

Just before I was to take my last exam, Hussain disappeared. Some speculated that he had run off to Bombay to be in films and laughed at his fecklessness. Others insisted that his father had killed and buried him, and that he might be found in a fallow field, or a ditch, or by the river. Nobody knew for sure. Some of the boys organized a search party and even equipped themselves with shovels and hoes for digging, but they were only boys and in the end, it was just another game they quickly tired of.

I don't know how, but perhaps it was the way that shame can cloak dark thoughts, or perhaps simply the sheer volume of chemical formulas crowding my brain, or the thrill of winning a scholarship abroad and the rushed preparations for my departure, but eventually I willed myself to forget about Hussain.

At the airport gate, my father placed a heavy hand on my shoulder and offered a few words of advice. "Do no harm," he had said. "Think carefully of the kind of man you want to be." I had heard a warning in the message, and had shuddered. What exactly did my father think of me?

With two degrees and an apartment now big enough for guests, I had sent airline tickets to my parents. My father had refused to come, offering no explanation. He never spoke to me on the phone either, only sent curt messages through my mother.

The meaning of the one-way ticket to Toronto my father had bought for me became clear. My father had renounced me, ashamed. "If your father won't go to visit you, then you come to visit us," my mother would plead, her voice scratchy with longing over the phoneline. Would she have stuck by me if she had known the truth about me? I spent nights wondering, tossing under my sheets, trying to blot out the lights of the big city where electricity was never shut off and the water was hot and flowed endlessly from chrome taps, and wherever I went, I could not avoid my own grim-faced reflection. And then one day, I sank into Canada, and to my surprise, Canada was an accommodating beanbag chair, politely rearranging its shape for my comfort.

Jai stood up and stamped his legs on the ground to bring back circulation into his legs. His children had returned from their voyage abroad, and their landing was a noisy and dusty one. Finally, their engines sputtered to a stop.

"*We're back. We're back. Did you miss us, pita-ji?*"

In response, Jai ruffled their hair. He looked at me, as if hoping I would love and pet his children too, but his children were wise and knew to flee to their mother. He flicked the stub of his *bidi* over the courtyard wall, as if my mother's wheat field was his personal ashtray. "I must say goodnight to the children." At the door to my mother's house, though, he hesitated before entering, turning his head my way, as if asking for permission. I grunted gruffly, and made a big show of lighting up another *bidi*. I was in no hurry to be reminded that my mother's house had been thoroughly, and permanently, colonized by others.

I had a sudden urge to go back, fly back in time to my mother's house, when it was hers and ours alone, and run through the open door, flinging my school books down on the walnut table in the small parlour room. I wanted to tell her about the small problems of my life: the lost or broken toy, the math teacher with his angry stinging cane, the dying deer Hussain and I had once found in the forest. I wanted to embrace her, feel her patting my head with her hands still gloved with flour from rolling the evening's chapathis. And at the same time, I wanted to hit her, hit my father. Lash out at the whole damn lot of them.

The next day I ventured out along the path I had taken decades ago to Hussain's house. The servants had been there earlier in the morning so I knew Hussain's mother was expecting my arrival. I had brought along some pakoras Neelum had made for me to take.

Hussain's mother exclaimed over me. She was stooped now with age, and much shorter than me, and so I knelt especially low as I touched her feet so she could pat me on the shoulder. Her toenails needed clipping. I gave her the gift I had brought, perfume, Chanel No. 5, which she exclaimed over, dabbing a little on her pulse. Then, she hid the bottle behind the bolster on her divan. That seemed odd, but I did not say anything about her unusual choice for storage. She begged me to sit down on the divan across from her so that she could talk with me.

"You were his good friend," she said. It was an acknowledgement of a long ago truth. I shifted uneasily in my seat.

"What has become of him?" I asked.

"He has become a movie actor in Bombay. He has made many, many movies," she said. She recited the names of several popular movies. I had seen them, sitting in the dark with Marcel, singing along to the video, laughing at the poorly translated English subtitles. I hadn't remembered seeing Hussain.

"You must be proud of him," I said, though puzzled. Surely I would have recognized Hussain if I had seen him in a movie.

"Yes, I am. I am very proud. Always proud." She got up and left the room, wiping her eyes with her *pallou*. I heard her move about in the dark kitchen, heard a propane tank being lit, perhaps for chai.

Hussain's father walked in, scraping his feet at the threshold and flicking his *chappals* off. The worn leather sandals landed several feet away, thwacking a ceramic jug of water kept full in case the tank on top of the house ran dry.

He squinted at me. "You are from abroad?" His question was a bark.

"Yes," I acknowledged warily. "I have come to ask after your wife and Hussain."

I was suddenly, irrationally, worried about the perfume bottle behind the bolster. What if he sat there and leaned against it? It would break and there would be a stink.

"Hussain?"

"Yes," I said. I tried to force my voice not to quiver as he advanced on me, lurching this way and that way. He was a barrel-chested, heavy-set man. His hair was grey, but despite his advanced years, I had no doubt he could take me down with one closed fist. I could smell the liquor on his breath, a smell like decomposing fruit, like mould growing on bread, like a million of life's irritations and a million more injustices crammed into one pipe bomb.

He stopped just a foot away from me. His eyes, yellow with jaundice or with liver disease, scanned my face trying to place me in time, then widened with recognition. "You are Mohan's son! You are the cause of all our misery," he yelled.

His wife came running into the room and then stopped abruptly, her hand shooting up to cover her mouth, but her words spilled out anyway. "Calm down," she cried, then waved her hands up and down, as if motioning for him to sit. "He has come all the way from Canada. Ca-na-da."

I had a sixth sense for danger, the cop decoys at the urinal at Bloor Station, the crackhead willing to do violence at a refusal for small change, the divorced chemist at work with the old and stained love letters from his wife kept next to a hunting knife at his drawer at work. But I didn't need my sixth sense to tell me I was in danger. I willed my feet to move. He didn't block my way, but he didn't move out of my way either. I passed around him, then bent to search for my *chappals* at the door's threshold. I could feel his hulking presence behind me, staring at my back. I hoped he would not kick me.

"Idiot, she," he said, as I slipped my *chappals* on quickly. "She probably tells you he's some big-big film star. But Hussain, he is dead. He ran away and never came back. No one has received *one iota* of a letter from him." He held up an index finger to emphasize his point. "No one has received *one iota* of a telegram. He must be dead. Don't believe otherwise." His index finger pointed, then fired in my direction. "You turned him bad. You turned him stupid."

In my hurry I had stuck my middle toe in the loop meant for the big toe, and my *chappal* slapped this way and that way as I hurried down the path. I could still hear Hussain's father yelling at his wife. "Stupid woman. Stupid like a goat."

A moment later, glass shattered at my heels, with a sound like that of hearts breaking. I could feel a shard bite into my left foot, and the scent of Chanel filled the air. He must have found the gift I had given Hussain's mother.

I smelled like a cosmetic department, like lilacs and talcum powder when I finally reached the courtyard gate of my mother's house, breathless. Jai and Neelum stood waiting for me, frowning in concert. Neelum held out a stainless steel tumbler of boiled water for me. I took it, thanking her profusely, touched by her kindness.

"It is my fault," Jai said. "I should have warned you. He is a very, very angry man. I tell my wife, 'It is best not to visit this home.'"

"What happened?" Neelum asked. "We could hear shouting even this far."

I paced about the courtyard, my feet kicking up a fine miasma of dust that hid my red face, my dishevelled being. "Stupid boy," his father had screamed as I walked away from his house. "No thought of his family." I could still hear the angry words he had hurled at my back.

My voice shaking, I told Jai and Neelum what had transpired, omitting the reference to his father's accusations about my responsibility in Hussain's disappearance.

Jai considered what I had told him, pulling at his ear as he spoke. "Yes, his mother thinks she has seen him in films. A bus driver, background only. But you should not put any weight in what she says. A mother's love," he said, shrugging. "She's not been well in her head since he left." Jai's head shook from side to side in sympathy.

Then Neelum spoke. "It is not just Mumbai that is so attractive. Here young boys go and join the militants, the *fiyadeen*." She pulled her shawl over her head and retreated into its cave, as if for safety. "Perhaps that is what he did." Her eyes scanned the mountains in the distance, as if looking for the insurgents and foreign mercenaries hidden in its crags and crevices. "This land is full of trouble."

I stopped pacing and stared at the sharp ridges of the steel grey mountains. It was a possibility I had never considered. Perhaps Hussain was lying in a shallow soldier's grave or rotting in a damp and mouldy

Indian prison cell. I shuddered. Then, I dismissed the idea. Hussain had cried that day we found the deer in a shallow depression in the forest, its leg broken, sweating in pain. "We should stay with her till she feels a bit better," he had said, stroking its back gingerly. He had been too sweet to ever pick up a gun or lob a petrol bomb, no matter how badly his father might have brutalized him. He would never have been like the men my father had secretly summoned who had ringed the hole and laughed as they pelted the doe with stones till it had finally moved on to a better life.

My last day in the village, the sun was swollen and rose heavily like an old woman labouring up a hill, tired of her earthly responsibilities. I held a private ceremony by the river with Neelum and Jai at my side. Jai patted my back as I held the large urn. The fragments of bones inside rattled as I shook while I said the words of goodbye. My mother's ashes formed a heavy film on the surface of the water before sinking, but a fine mist of her blew back over me, clinging to my eyelashes. There was nothing I could do but wipe her away along with my tears.

What had happened to Hussain was a mystery I lugged back to Delhi with me, where I stayed in a hotel in the exclusive inner ring of Connaught Circle. While waiting for my flight out the next day, I visited Palika Bazaar, an underground shopping concourse designed to outsmart the blistering sun, but I had no desire to trawl the shops for trinkets or for men.

Normally I liked mysteries. I liked riddles, the Sunday crosswords, the cryptograms, the word games I puzzled out on my king-size bed with the patchwork quilt from India my mother had sent when I bought my first house in North Toronto. An executive house, the ad had said. Marcel, relaxed, read the sports section, a Sunday kind of satisfied in his terry cloth robe made fragrant by the sandalwood incense I always kept burning in the bathroom. I missed Marcel, though he was only a cell call away, working on his never-ending dissertation about the history of the cane workers in St. Lucia.

Inside my hotel room, the plush white coverlet seduced me. I dozed though it was morning, and dreamt of my mother patting my knee.

She was wrapped in the white of widowhood, though in the dream her hair was not shorn. "Why are you always running? First, you ran from us and never came back, now you run from Marcel though he loves you."

In the dream, I sobbed with relief that my mother knew of my relationship with Marcel and didn't mind my love for a man. I sobbed at the pain of never having returned, of never having seen her again. My mother continued, still patting me on my knee, "Why do you run from little boys who need a kind friend?" Her hand reached higher and higher, until she found my penis.

I woke up, my armpits slimy with cold sweat. I got up and paced the marble floor in a daze till my mind finally latched onto the cell phone in my rucksack.

When Marcel answered the phone, I willed myself to sit on my bed in Toronto, to imagine Marcel's ever-present papers and articles, their metal staples sticking into my flesh. Marcel was excited to hear from me, his voice seeming to sing as it bounced through the atmosphere from satellite to receiver.

"All your plants are fine. I've been taking good care of them. As for me, I've had quite a spurt of writing, finished three chapters since you've gone. If you stay away just a few more weeks, I'll have done with this awful thesis of mine and we can finally celebrate my ascension to the academic throne."

So Marcel had been occupied with his thesis and not with other men. Longing for Marcel surged through my body.

"What's wrong, baby?" Marcel asked. I had intended not to tell him of Hussain and of his father's tirade; I wanted to forget it all. But I found myself telling him everything.

"Is there any other way you could find out what happened to him?" Marcel asked. He was a researcher after all.

"What? Go to Bombay, inquire at the talent agencies?!" I laughed at my own suggestion, at how idiotic it sounded.

"Why not?"

"What if he died with a gun in his hands fighting with the Hizbul Mujahideen? Or what if he's not in Bombay at all — what if his father really did kill him?"

"You know, it's funny," Marcel said, the way he always did before he told a story about back home. "There was this boy in St. Lucia they terrorized when I was a kid, probably gay. They used to back him right up against the sugar canes and threaten him with machetes. I thought for sure he must have died young, murdered or by suicide. Then I saw him when I went back. He owned a paddle boat rental business, complete with goggles and fins."

I could see Marcel's gay boatman at his shed, sipping rum at the counter while politely fending off flirty white girls in string bikinis. Why could he stay and make a life for himself when I couldn't? Why was I doomed to be the stay-away boy, glued to another country solely because of the certainty of rejection in this one? It was too much. Everything in my life had been thwarted. Thwarted lust for Hussain, thwarted returns. I would never be the prodigal son returned. I would never again have a moment as perfect as the day in the fields with my kite billowing behind me and the perfect love of my parents. Only my mother had not rejected me — but she had never known me, the excited boy in the storeroom, the boy in sexual bloom, the boy I had to leave behind.

Do no harm, my father had said. Had I done harm, by doing nothing for Hussain? Had I done harm to my parents, especially my mother, by staying away?

What did I owe them? Hadn't I, myself, been saved from harm a million times — by the tiny gestures of my mother, who endured my years of rebuff and never severed her connection, by that one action of my father, who sent me abroad, as a way to be rid of me, for sure, but maybe also as a convoluted, though perverted, form of protection, and by the many interventions of Marcel who had stopped me from excess drinking over and over again?

I sat on the phone in silence. Marcel knew me, knew what my silences meant. He murmured soothing endearments.

"Maybe if I go to Bombay I might find him," I said, miserable.

"Maybe," Marcel said, a tumultuous pity in his voice.

"Will you still be there when I get back?" I asked my lover.

Marcel didn't answer my question. "Change your flight. Go find Hussain," he said, "or a trace of him, and if that's not possible, then a story about him that you can live with, that can allow you to sleep at night."

In Bombay, I couldn't help myself. The Gateway of India was tall and arched as if expecting giants, and my own hopes stretched as I passed through it. While I strolled the boardwalk by the sea wall, I scanned the passersby for Hussain. I went to the cinema, settled into plush red velvet seats and drank in film after film. As the camera panned the bustling metropolis of Bombay, streets so busy you could lose yourself and disappear entirely, I studied the actors. The hero always wore dark sunglasses and rode a scooter or motorcycle, dodging bullock carts, street vendors and any three-wheeled taxis blocking his way, all the while singing. I looked for Hussain in every scene, in the faces of the extras, the businessman getting into an Ambassador, the vendor at his pushcart selling spicy *channa* in rolled up newspaper cones, the beggar in grey rags on the street corner, the saddhu covered in white paste. I wrote down the name of the production companies and tried to contact them.

"Sir, many actors we are using," one secretary said in Bombay English, flitting from English to Hindi and back again. "We don't keep records so far back and many people do not use their real names. Still much shame to be in this business."

I tried the government records, the lists of the dead. The austere government buildings, their over-curious clerks and infuriating snail-paced records searches turned up nothing. It was as if Hussain had disappeared off the face of the earth.

I returned, deflated, to my empty hotel room. I snapped and unsnapped the latches on my suitcases while the overhead fan spun endlessly in its tightly controlled orbit, taunting me. I had come full circle, and still I had no answers.

Since my father's rejection, I had practised never looking back — just down the narrow view of deep glasses full of vodka, of rum. Here, now, I was looking, but I couldn't find the one thing, the one person I wanted to see. I thought about what Vedic philosophy had to say about life — I didn't remember my early lessons clearly, but I remembered there were four stages, the last one a duty to the spiritual life, to introspection and reflection.

Was this how I was going to spend the remaining parts of my life: ruminating over lost things, lost love? Would it be all recriminations and remorse? Was I going to spend my life wondering about Hussain, angry that I had not spoken to him, had rejected him that day in the schoolyard? If I had taken his face in my hand and kissed him, his cut and bruised lips, would our lives have unfolded any differently?

Exhausted, I lay in bed and stared at the walls, but they remained stubbornly blank. Just as I tumbled into a deep sleep, I felt a familiar sensation: the butterfly weight of a hand alighting on my shoulder and the soft kiss of silk tickling my cheek. I forced my eyes open, hoping to catch one last glimpse of my mother, and though I didn't quite see her, I thought I saw the flicker of a shadow cross the walls. It could have been her. It could have been anything, a gecko scurrying in front of a lamp, the tips of my own eyelashes, but if we can make of shadows what we will, it gave me a certain peace to think that I saw the silhouette of a woman, her *dupatta* billowing behind her.

Though it was very early in the morning in Toronto, I called Marcel on my cellphone. I was ensconced in a black taxi and on my way to the airport. I had made a decision. Even if I couldn't make love stick this time, I would die trying.

"I want to bring you to India," I said to my lover, who had answered the phone groggy and gruff with sleep. It was a declaration of sorts.

"That would be wonderful," Marcel said, his voice clearing with awakening and surprise. I could hear the sheets rustle, the springs squeak. Was Marcel jumping up and down?

"Yes, on a honeymoon," I clarified, taking a risk.

"Oh!"

"Yes, maybe we could go to Kashmir, where all the couples go to honeymoon. You just have to see Srinagar."

"I have to see Srinagar! Absolutely, I have to see Srinagar!"

I could hear the sound of clapping. I was delighted with Marcel's response.

As my plane hurtled towards Marcel, I planned our trip on the back of a napkin until the lights in the jumbo airliner dimmed. The screen several rows in front of me lit up, a colourful Bombay street scene, another Bollywood gangster film. It was curious, maybe a trick of alcohol or of the high altitude, but I thought everyone seemed to bear a faint resemblance to Hussain. Just before the credits rolled I blew loud kisses to all the boys on the screen, and even the ladies in their crisp saris giggling in the row beside me and covering their peanut-salted mouths with their hands couldn't stop me.

HIGH REGARDS

I

ANIL HOVERED BY THE RADIO OPERATOR'S SIDE, ANXIOUS TO HEAR THE reports from Sector 10 before the coming storm made transmissions impossible. Finally, the set crackled and hissed, and the operator sprang to work, one hand cupping his headset against his ear, and the other adjusting the black knobs to eliminate the static.

"Chakravorti." The operator scribbled down the name, and then the details. Anil watched the blue ink spreading its stain across the page. Pradeep, his friend, the paramedic on the helicopter, was relaying the nature of the injuries: a possible fracture to the right radius, a broken tibia, possible broken ribs and a possible concussion.

Anil did not even finish reading the notes, rushing instead to the infirmary to prepare for the injured soldier. He loaded the film into the X-ray equipment, slit open bags of plaster of Paris, laid strips of white gauze to sun under the bright lights of the operating room on stainless steel trays, and garlanded transparent bags of saline and antibiotic solutions around metal poles. He imagined this was the procedure the previous doctors had followed, and wondered again at the short-term nature of their stays at this base camp.

After two months of confinement to a mountain ledge not more than half a mile deep, he himself was starting to feel a bit restless and a touch claustrophobic. As a boy, he had imagined life in the army differently, a life with dangerous vistas — the view from the top of a charging elephant, the spinning turret of a firing tank, the exposed glass eye of a fighter jet alight with pyrotechnics — not this confinement to a single location, despite its spectacular views of the Pir Panjal, its proximity to the disputed Line of Control where all the action was.

From the barred windows of his infirmary Anil watched for the helicopter. Finally it came, bursting through a black cloud and looping over the mountain crags to hover over the helipad before settling in, like a pregnant woman lowering herself onto a divan. The winds were slamming fists that jolted the helicopter from side to side until it fishtailed suddenly, scattering ground crew. Anil, despite the flutter of excitement he felt with every delivery, worried for the injured soldier, worried for his friend Pradeep.

Anil had become fond of Pradeep, the tall and bony paramedic, absent-minded on the ground but sharp as a hawk in the air, a decade of experience evident in his accurate calls. Anil admired Pradeep's passion for flight and the way he flaunted army protocol by wearing his hair long and in a ponytail. Most of all, he appreciated that Pradeep didn't treat him as the others did because of his status, the General's favourite nephew, as if he were a delicate porcelain doll to be admired but kept tucked away high on a shelf, out of harm's way. On Anil's first day on the mountain, Pradeep promised he would take him where the action was once Anil had acclimatized to mountain life. Until then, Anil contented himself by listening attentively to Pradeep's fanciful and poetic descriptions of his flights.

"How was the ride today?" he would ask, and Pradeep might reply, "We were so high in the air, I could feel the clouds brush my kneecaps."

Sometimes he would toss his wool cap in the air and it would drop on the floor. Anil would retrieve it for him. Despite his greater rank as a doctor, Anil always deferred to Pradeep.

"The engine stalled, and we dropped two hundred feet in a milli-second. My eyelids turned inside out," Pradeep might say and Anil would feel the drop in the pit of his own stomach. Or, "K8 is waking. It'll be shaking off its winter coat very soon," and Anil would make a note to prepare for more incoming avalanche related accidents. Or, "The black clouds followed us for miles before pouncing on us. We had to turn back. Poor bugger who shot his own toes will just have to wait." Anil would commiserate with Pradeep then, in the canteen, over rice and dhal, about the power of nature to determine man's fate.

Before the helicopter pilot had even cut the engine, Pradeep sprang out.
Anil could see him crouching beneath the whirling blades, motioning
to those inside to hurry, but the soldiers from Sector 10 took their time
disembarking. Pradeep shouted into the maw of the helicopter. Finally,
the soldiers ambled past Pradeep, lugging a wooden stretcher between
them, the injured soldier on it listing dangerously to one side.

Anil noted that the wind from the helicopters' angry arms had swept
the shiny silver warming blanket half off the soldier's body, and it dangled
like peeling skin onto the helipad. Nobody thought to stop to re-cover
him, certainly not his comrades who sauntered along the short path to
the infirmary, deposited him in the examination room and left without a
backward look. Anil wondered at their disregard for their fellow soldier,
but held his tongue. If his uncle had witnessed this display, he was sure
they, and their Commanding Officer, would have been given a tongue-
lashing and sent to clean the latrines, but Anil had become careful about
mentioning his uncle's name in front of Pradeep. It had been the only
sore point in their easy friendship.

Anil's first assessment of the unconscious Chakravorti was that he was
young, perhaps twenty years of age, and that he was Bengali, the sun
of the Deccan valley still evident in his face despite his wintry post.
Pradeep, Anil noted, had failed to mention the bloody and swollen
nose or the multiple bruises on the soldier's face. It was clear that
this was no ordinary accident of a high-altitude war. The munitions
storehouse had not exploded, sending pieces of metal of all sizes and
shapes through soft tissue, flinging spears of burning timber helter-
skelter. Pakistan had not shot at them with AK-47s or American-made
heat-seeking missiles, there were no gunshot wounds, no evisceration
of stomach, no limb dangling only by a thread of sinew. There were
no compression fractures from being buried alive in an avalanche, no
edema to the lungs or frostbite earned while waiting to be excavated.
No, this was something else entirely.

Pradeep burst into the examination room while Anil was palpating
the soldier's liver for swelling. Pradeep signed a form before unclipping

it from his pad and put it on the wooden stool beside the makeshift lab. Together, they positioned the young man on the X-ray table and Anil listened attentively as Pradeep delivered his report.

On his short stay on the mountain, Pradeep narrated, Chakravorti had been assigned as an inventory clerk, posted outside the munitions storehouse, a tin shed draped with twigs for camouflage and encircled by a halo of barbed wire and sandbags. "The CO says he's O positive. Except for the possible internal bleeding, I doubt you'll need to send him down."

"Down" was the hill station in Baltal, where there was a proper hospital for convalescing. "How did he come by these injuries?" Anil asked, peeling off the blood-tinged pad to examine Chakravorti's right eye.

Pradeep shrugged. "Who can say?"

Anil resumed his examination of Chakravorti.

A small explosion beside his right ear made Anil drop the gauze. It was Pradeep, banging his metal clipboard against the wall. His violent response surprised Anil. Pradeep practised detachment, and usually remained indifferent to the human suffering he airlifted in.

"Insolent bastards. They should all be court-martialled," Pradeep growled.

"What does the Commanding Officer say?" Anil said, alarmed.

"DeSousa? You can speak to him yourself, he came down with us," Pradeep said. "No doubt, he'll tell you the usual."

"The usual?" Anil was puzzled.

"Oh, that it was mountain madness," Pradeep explained.

DeSousa was a portly man in his late thirties, with a receding hairline and a bad case of rosacea on his bulbous nose. He had begrudgingly consented to Anil's request for an interview because, Anil supposed, nobody wanted to risk angering the only doctor thousands and thousands of feet above sea level. DeSousa sat perched on the edge of the metal folding chair in Anil's tiny office, a closet-like space that held the standard army furniture — one metal desk, two chairs, a single stool and a filing cabinet.

Anil had asked Pradeep to join him in his questioning of the

Commanding Officer, but Pradeep remained silent, standing in the corner by the file cabinet, picking at its peeling paint. "Permission to speak freely, Sir?" Anil asked.

DeSousa nodded his assent.

"Chakravorti's injuries certainly are numerous," Anil said. "What happened here?"

DeSousa took his time before answering. He had the focused air Anil had seen on his uncle's face when he played chess, his mind calculating odds and probabilities, the wisdom of a particular move. "Chakravorti's injuries were received while he was being restrained for theft of army supplies," DeSousa finally explained.

"A broken leg? A broken radius? Contusions to the face? Come now!" Anil said, his eyebrows dancing up. His voice became high-pitched when he was excited, and his cheeks coloured when he heard his own voice. He wanted to appear manly, not young, though he was barely twenty, probably just a year or two younger than his patient. He forced himself to focus back on Chakravorti. He had left him in the recovery room, entombed in his new white plaster armour, a morphine drip leaking into his arm, black criss-cross stitches marking his face. The X-rays had revealed the expected, three broken bones, as well as the unexpected — many older breaks, some badly set. Anil had counted them, and when he had told Pradeep of their number and location, Pradeep had only shrugged, as if he had expected it.

"The men got a little carried away, perhaps. The Rao fellow is a hothead." DeSousa stirred in his chair, thumping the floorboards with his boots as if trying to shake loose some snow. "These postings at the top of the mountain, they drive you mad. The cold up here is not refreshing. The men are always so afraid of avalanches, mortar shells, missile attacks. Even afraid to go outside to the latrine during a blizzard, thinking they'll fall off the mountain's edge. And there's not much to do, really. They pick at each other."

"Still," Anil said. He chose his next words carefully. "We're all brothers here, we should not be fighting with each other."

"Hmm." DeSousa nodded, as if agreeing. "Here's my memo for his file." He stood up and handed the paper to Pradeep, over Anil's head. "I must go back to my men now."

Anil winced at the disrespect.

"You see. As I said, a total waste of time." Pradeep plopped himself down on the stool.

"I don't believe him," Anil said, staring out the window at DeSousa lumbering down the path towards the canteen. "Not a word."

"Does it really matter what you believe?" Pradeep swung his leg off the wooden stool and marched off to the radio room to listen for incoming calls. Anil listened to his footsteps fade. His heart had skipped a few beats with Pradeep's harsh words, but Anil reassured himself that this was only a minor disagreement, and it would pass. He turned his attention to the X-rays in Chakravorti's file.

From the time Anil was in short pants, riding in his uncle's jeep, he had known he would follow his uncle into the army. His parents had not even questioned his choice, too preoccupied with financing his older sisters' marriages. Their hair had turned grey with worry about promissory banknotes and second mortgages, and the exorbitant cost of stocking their future in-law's houses with refrigerators, blenders and all manner of electrical appliances. There was no one to guide Anil until his uncle had driven up in his general's jeep to shepherd him into the right career choice.

Anil had dreamed of being a soldier, dreamed of the day he would leave his tin soldiers and plastic action figures behind in the dust of his parent's courtyard and enter the real encampments of brave men. He loved the textures of war: its heavy canvas, the gleaming metal poles, the rough ropes tied to stakes. He loved the sound of war: the roar of jeeps, the whine of fighter jets, the thunderous explosion of bombs. Neatly made cots, rows of polished black boots and shining silver trunks excited him. Most of all, he admired the orderliness of the army, the honesty of its pecking order, the clarity of its objectives.

"For his training as a doctor he has to return five years of service, then he's free to do as he wishes," Rahul Uncle had advised Anil's parents.

"But Uncle-ji, I don't want to be an army doctor, I want to be a soldier," Anil had protested, his voice cracking with the effort of keeping his indignation in check.

Rahul Uncle had laughed heartily and ignored him.

"But with all this trouble in Kashmir will he be safe?" His mother wrapped the *pallou* of her sari more tightly around her lithe frame, a nervous habit, one that made Anil think of a caterpillar winding a silky cocoon around itself. His father looked down onto the concrete floor and studied its fine cracks as if he was reading an astrology chart that predicted Anil's future, before finally giving his assent.

His uncle reassured his parents, "No need to worry, he'll only know base camps, safe from fighting. I promise this, on my own head. After all, he is like my own son."

The day was warm and filled with the sonorous clap of snow thunder as heavy shelves of snow cleaved apart and tumbled off the mountain. Anil unzipped his down-filled parka and trudged towards the infirmary, away from the canteen where he had burnt the tip of his tongue on too-hot chai. Reflexively, he kept his head tilted up, hyper-vigilant to avalanches, but his thoughts were of his new patient, Chakravorti.

The infirmary was a metal shack outfitted with ten cots, and a surgical room that was swabbed three times a day with a pungent heavy-duty disinfectant. His patient lay on the cot nearest the heater, on a morphine drip for his pain. He was conscious in the way the drugged can sometimes be, his head turning towards the sounds of approaching footsteps, but his eyes remaining closed, sometimes fluttering as if dreaming. He was still running a low-grade fever, which Anil duly noted on the chart at the foot of the bed. Anil sat beside him and dabbed his patient's lips with a water-laden sponge.

Pradeep entered the room, and nodded to Anil. He took a quick look at the chart, too, and then held Chakravorti's wrist, checking his pulse. The young soldier awoke at the touch, his eyelids fluttering, the dark hole of his pupils expanding and contracting while trying to fix on the medic.

"I didn't die?" he asked. He coughed, a rattling sound, and Anil wondered if he had developed pneumonia overnight.

"No. You're here at base camp, in the infirmary. Do you remember what happened?" Pradeep asked.

"It's better that I should have died." Chakravorti turned his head away.

Pradeep didn't appear shocked. Anil knew there had been a handful of suicides and many more attempts in Pradeep's ten years of service as a medic. The last one had been a twenty-year-old boy from Assam, who had jumped in front of a two-tonne lorry. The one before, an eighteen-year-old boy from Delhi, had thrown himself over the edge of a mountain cliff.

"Why do you say that?" Pradeep held Chakravorti's hand and patted it with his own.

Chakravorti closed his eyes and sighed.

Anil wished the boy would cry. He welcomed the weepy release of soldiers, their unabashed sobbing, their relief at being finally safe in a base camp, at least for a while. Because after they cried, a temporary peace usually enveloped them. It made his job easier, writing the note that sent them back to the Line again. But Chakravorti fell asleep, his cheeks dry as the Rajasthani desert.

The boy was too young to be so broken, Anil thought. No body should contain so many broken bones, reveal such a history of pain and suffering. His vulnerability, his despair, angered Anil. Someone, a fellow soldier, had beaten him, and should pay for that. This was not the way the army should be run.

Anil said goodbye to Pradeep and strode into the next building, the main administration building.

"Have the Records Department pull all of Chakravorti's files," he said to the clerk.

"All?" the clerk queried.

"That's what I said."

When the files finally appeared on his desk, the thick piles of memos secreted within them surprised Anil. When he read the contents, Anil decided to place a radio call to his uncle, despite what Pradeep might think about his connections.

II

On his school breaks, Anil had often visited his uncle in Mussoorie, the hill town with two faces.

One face of Mussoorie was its public side, a pretty enclave of luxury hotels and European buildings, at its centre a promenade where most of the town's activity took place. The cantonment section of Mussoorie was its other face, containing officer's residences and a sprawling army base, barracks for soldiers, warehouses for tanks, trucks, jeeps and buses, tents, kitchen equipment, endless piles of munitions and boxes of files, all locked in warehouses with heavy steel doors and no windows.

His parents told him they were sending him to his uncle so that his aunt's maternal urges could be appeased. Lata Auntie had never been able to have children and, Anil had heard his mother whispering to his other aunts, wept copiously when she bled each month. But when Anil arrived, she studiously ignored him, and it was Uncle Rahul who doted on him instead. His uncle was the one who ensured that the cook prepared his favourite foods, boneless chicken and biryani with loads and loads of cashews. He was the one who took him on his ambles along the promenade, suggesting a ride up the rope-way cable car to Gun Hill where they could stare, all day, at the snow-clad peaks of the Western Garhwal or down into the fertile Dehradun Valley below. It was his uncle whose maternal needs seemed to be appeased each time Anil arrived.

At the time, Anil's uncle was a general in the Western Command on special assignment to the Kashmir region. He commanded his own jeep and driver. It was rumoured that he was on the fast track for promotion, and possible consideration for work abroad, perhaps a diplomatic assignment.

Anil knew that his uncle was not only a successful man, but a well-respected one. Anil had seen the letters relatives had written his uncle, asking for advice on everything from expanding their businesses, to best train routes for travel, to educational choices for their children. Anil had been proud of his uncle, proud that he was his uncle's favourite nephew, and often bragged to his school friends about his stays in Mussoorie. Once a new boy from Delhi had joined their form and within two days had fought six boys. Anil had been terrified of him, and when the boy had cornered him in the yard demanding money, Anil had peed in his pants. After that, Anil always made sure strangers knew right away who his uncle was and just how many soldiers with guns his uncle commanded. He went to sleep praying that he, too, would one day be as respected and feared as his uncle was.

Chakravorti's file sat on Anil's desk. He had been shunted from post to post in and around Srinagar and then into the deep valleys of Kashmir's remote villages. The first injury happened when he had been with a battalion sent to flush insurgents out of villages in the north-western sector, an area protected from logging and noted for its apple, apricot and walnut orchards.

The accident had been minor, a gunshot wound to his lower right leg — friendly fire, the chart noted. Nevertheless, Chakravorti had been transferred to a nearby battalion upon recovery. There he sustained injuries consistent with a beating: broken ribs, contusions to his head, broken teeth, significant bruising. The young soldier had experienced seven accidents before his assignment to Sector 10, and had been transferred six times. The chart noted the suspicious injuries, but no explanatory memoranda accompanied it. The rest of the accidents were consistent with beatings. Anil traced his index finger lightly over Chakravorti's X-ray image, as if Chakravorti's body was a map of Kashmir. He could stop at each break, and map it to a village destroyed. He could now say, "this beating happened in Uri, this one in Srinagar." Then Anil had found a memo from his uncle in the pile.

"Uncle-ji, I have a problem I hope you can help me with," Anil said to his uncle over the microphone in the radio room, his eyes fixed on the memo before him.

"For you, anything," his uncle said.

Anil recounted Chakravorti's injuries to his uncle. His uncle listened without interruption. "You were responsible for the headquarters in Srinagar when two soldiers were shot by our own soldiers, no?"

His uncle took his time responding. "Ah yes, that dirty affair," he finally said. "It was a logging scandal. Stupid officers were offering protection to illegal loggers for a payoff. They shot anyone who wouldn't keep their mouths closed. They killed their own men, but claimed they were deaths due to 'friendly fire.' The officers were court-martialled."

"I have one of your friendly fire men here," Anil said. "Chakravorti."

"Chakravorti? Yes, I remember him. Slight fellow, very young? Lucky to be alive, the other soldier was killed, you know."

"He's had many accidents since then with suspicious injuries, in-juries consistent with beatings. Now he's in my infirmary with more suspicious injuries."

His uncle sighed audibly over the hiss and crackle of the radio. Anil wanted his uncle to deny any involvement in Chakravorti's situation, but how could he? He was responsible for the sector.

"But, *beta,* what can I do for you? I only know about the Srinagar affair." Anil noted with dismay a defensive tone to his uncle's voice.

"Could this beating be related to the Srinagar affair?" Anil persisted anyway.

"Could be. Many of the officers involved were demoted and transferred to the Line. They could have stuck tight, holding a grudge, afraid this soldier might point the finger at them."

"But you authorized all transfers didn't you?" Anil could hear his own voice, tentative, almost apologetic.

"Look, *beta,* you are making wild speculations without knowing a thing. Why don't you ask Chakravorti himself what happened. Only this way will you know the truth. I personally have no use for Rambos like the ones who shot at your man. Get him to talk if you can, but I don't think you will have much success."

"I'll get him to talk," Anil vowed and flipped the switch to end their communication. Anil hoped that his uncle was as ignorant of the Chakravorti case as he claimed. Any scandals erupting at this time would be bad for his uncle, with tension flaring up at the border again.

The wind outside had picked up, rattling the tin roof of the infirmary, the camouflage net of twigs scraping and thumping against it.

"Maybe the tiger will stop hunting the doe, too." Pradeep had laughed at his uncle's suggestion. "If Chakravorti talks, they *will* kill him," he said more soberly.

"Can we at least send him home?" Anil asked, feeling his inexperience creep out from behind his white medical coat to sit between them, naked. Two months on a mountain! And he was fighting with Commanding Officers? Was he mad? Did he have mountain madness himself? Anil took a deep breath, calmed himself down and continued with his thought. "A medical discharge, maybe?"

"His injuries will heal in a month or two, you can't get a medical discharge for that. And he has three years left of service." Pradeep rifled through Chakravorti's file, reading. "He was trained as a munitions technician."

Anil understood, finally, the meaning of his own contract with the army. Now that he, like Chakravorti, had finished his training, he had become an investment. They would be indebted till they had paid the army off in the agreed number of years of service.

"Can we counsel him to desert?" Anil asked Pradeep, whispering, afraid. Was it treason to counsel a soldier to desert, he wondered?

"You counsel him. Unlikely he will, since he hasn't already despite six beatings. His mother probably depends on his salary for her rice and dhal."

And then it dawned on Anil. "Poor bastard. He can't desert, can't even kill himself. His only hope is to be killed. At least his family will get a pension, then."

Three days after Chakravorti had first arrived he was finally awake and alert enough to carry on a conversation. Pradeep and Anil sat on either side of him.

"Water?" Chakravorti said. Pradeep sprang from his stool and rushed to the sink, fretting through cupboards for the paper cups.

"Who did this to you?" Anil asked, tapping gently on the white cast encasing Chakravorti's left leg.

"Nobody did this to me." He strained to rise, but the weight of the sheets holding him down proved too much for him. "Let me alone."

Anil ignored Chakravorti's protestations.

"We can't do that. You must tell us who did this to you." Anil offered him the stainless steel cup, Anil's own, that Pradeep had found.

"Was it because of what happened in the northwestern sector?"

"No," the patient said, and his right hand found its way to his left, also encased in a cast. He stroked the top of the cast gently, as if surprised by its presence.

"So, it was about something else?" Anil prodded.

"Nobody's fault. Please, leave me be."

Chakravorti groaned as he tried to turn his body away from Anil, but Pradeep had returned to the other side, and now they were flanking him on both sides. Quickly, so quickly, Anil realized they had become interrogators.

"I have a better idea. Pradeep, let him rest alone, as he wishes." Anil strode out of the room.

Anil, though on the short side, had a sprinter's body, thin and wiry. He navigated the snow-encrusted pathways to the canteen with ease, though the winds were strong, rattling metal bunkers and pushing heavy equipment about. More than once, he had to stop suddenly and dig his boots with their metal crampons deep into the ice to avoid walking into the path of a cart or small bulldozer sliding by. He realized with relief tinged with pleasure that Pradeep had followed, loping through the snow after him.

As he approached the metal bunker where the canteen was housed, wind shears stabbed about the camp nearly tearing the door off its hinges when Anil opened it. On the roof overhead, the Indian flag seemed alarmed, too, snapping violently and yanking at its chains, as if trying to escape the coming storm.

Anil sighted KC Rao smoking cigarettes with the other soldiers from Sector 10. The "hothead," DeSousa had called him, the man who had "restrained" Chakravorti. Anil moved towards his target but almost abandoned his plan when he spotted DeSousa nearby at the officer's table. Yes, he was a doctor, and yes, special allowances were made for him because of that and because of his uncle, but any disrespect directed at DeSousa could still get him thrown in prison. He would have to be very careful.

"So you beat Chakravorti?" Anil pointed his finger at KC Rao. He gathered his courage. "He is very near death. If he dies, you'll all be facing a murder charge." He leaned close and whispered, "DeSousa won't be able to protect you then." He felt the charge of his words blast through KC Rao. DeSousa was throwing ferocious glances their way, as if warning against any confessions.

"Chakravorti's a liar," KC Rao said.

Anil smiled. Rao had taken the bait. He turned his back on the soldier, as if indifferent, and then stomped to the infirmary as he had come, exhilarated like a schoolboy who had just thrown his only stone at a bully. It took all his energy not to look back.

"What have you done?" Pradeep said, hurrying after him, looking over his shoulder as if he expected the entire squadron to burst through the door to deliver a beating to them both. "Aren't you afraid?"

Anil sat on his metal desk chair, his head between his legs, hit by a sudden wave of nausea.

"Of what?" he looked up at Pradeed. "Hotheads and idiots?"

"Hotheads with guns," Pradeep shouted at Anil.

"No. I'm not afraid of them," Anil shouted back, lying.

"Oh, I guess you have your uncle to save you from any trouble," Pradeep said.

Pradeep's jab stung. The silence between them was as stiff and inflammable as dry straw.

Pradeep looked out the window. "Here he comes."

KC Rao stood before them, a little sheepish. "I did nothing wrong," he said. "I followed orders. I didn't want to. I quite liked Chakravorti, but it was either him or me."

"So what's the game?" Pradeep asked. "Drugs? Ammunition?"

"Both."

Anil was reluctant to ask. He really didn't know what they were talking about. "Will somebody please explain what's going on?" he finally said.

KC Rao was only too willing to explain himself. "DeSousa sells our small arms to traffickers who sell them on to others. Then we blow up the storehouse, saying mortar shells have hit it, so nobody can do a proper count, you see. Same with drugs, the morphine and other painkillers at the camp."

"Why beat up Chakravorti?" Anil said.

"I thought he told you." KC Rao fidgeted with his belt buckle.

"He did tell us. You tell us your side," Anil said.

"He's been stealing the morphine. He likes it too much, you see. We were running low-low. Chakravorti didn't want them to take the morphine. He said it was his."

"You beat a man for a few drops of morphine?" Anil said, surprised.

"He asked for it this time, crazy bugger. When he couldn't take the withdrawal anymore, he went crazy, begged us to send him down here so he could steal some from your bigger supply. DeSousa agreed, but said it had to look real. He ordered me to beat him, but then he joined in. DeSousa's a lunatic."

Anil was shocked. He had been expecting another story. How Chakravorti had stood up to the corrupt officer, how he had been beaten to silence him from speaking out against corruption. He wasn't sure if he believed Petty Officer KC Rao.

"And the other times, the other beatings?"

"You must ask DeSousa about that," Rao said, a sneer crossing his face.

"Why confess to this beating, then? Aren't you afraid of telling on DeSousa?" Anil challenged him, feeling the stirrings of an irrational anger.

KC Rao looked at his polished boots as if they might help him walk away from the mess he had participated in. "A murder charge is very serious."

"You're lying for DeSousa, aren't you?" Anil said, but KC Rao just shrugged.

The wind had picked up again and the clatter above them sounded like an old fashioned war, thousands of horse hoofs thundering in battle.

"We'll see what Chakravorti has to say, then," Anil said.

"You said he had told you everything!" KC Rao said, outraged, and a string of invectives followed. To Anil's surprise — he had not expected Pradeep to back him up so fully — Pradeep escorted Petty Officer KC Rao out the door of his office, past the infirmary where Chakravorti lay, and deposited him in a snowdrift to cool off.

When they returned to the infirmary, Chakravorti was lying peacefully in his cot. Anil checked the morphine drip, not wanting to believe KC Rao's story. But, Anil noted with dismay, someone had increased the speed of the drip, effectively increasing the dosage. Looking out the window, Anil spotted KC Rao and a few soldiers milling about the infirmary's north face, smoking *bidis*.

"Maybe DeSousa did this?" Anil said to Pradeep, hoping Pradeep might agree.

"I doubt it. I heard no one come in. We would have heard them with these loose floorboards."

Chakravorti wasn't a victim of corruption, just a petty thief, an addict, stealing morphine meant for the brave soldiers injured defending their country. The realization made Anil angry. "He's trying to kill himself, then?" Anil asked, but doubted that Chakravorti would die. If he was addicted, the increased dosage was probably not an attempt at an overdose, but rather, a way to get relief.

A *jawan* burst into the recovery room with news. There was trouble again in Sector 10. "Sir, the radio operator suggested the doctor go, too."

Pradeep snorted. "Don't be ridiculous. He's to stay here, safe at base camp." He turned to Anil, "Don't go stirring up any more hornets' nests while I'm gone." Pradeep marched off without saying goodbye, eager to step into his helicopter and take refuge from earthly trouble.

III

Later, Anil would imagine that flight, again and again. The approach to Sector 10, treacherous. The winds picking up, slamming the helicopter up and away from the makeshift pad, and men rushing about as best as they could, weighed down by heavy parkas and snowboots. Pradeep's view from behind the glass eye of the strange flying insect he inhabited like a second skin, the missile launcher positioned between crags. And then the flare as the launcher shot its metal wad. Had the enemy infiltrated Sector 10? And then Pradeep's sudden realization as his helicopter was hit. Hit by their own. The pilot struggling for control. Pradeep sniffing a fuel leak, a terrible stinging in his nostrils. And the wall of the mountain, as blank as his future, looming up to greet him.

Anil tossed in his cot, besieged by images of Pradeep trapped in a glass bell jar, shouting something, but no matter how hard Anil tried he could not make out what Pradeep was saying. He couldn't sleep because every sound was a threat — the creak of a floorboard, the ricochet of ice pellets on the window, the explosive whoosh of an engine. He had to get out. He had placed a radio call to his uncle earlier, pushing the radio operator aside, but couldn't remember what he had said to him, only knew that his uncle was on his way.

Hours and hours passed, but finally, his uncle arrived, followed by his *jawan*. The *jawan* placed a tea tray on top of Anil's tin trunk at the foot of his cot. Anil refused the tea, and the toast already covered with marmalade his uncle proffered. He got up and paced the room.

"Put some clothes on at least," his uncle said. "You'll catch your death of cold."

Anil's white coat and shirt and wool trousers were spread out on the floor. He hadn't remembered taking off his clothes. The floor was cold, and he thought about getting dressed, but he was distracted by a vague memory.

After he had been told the news he screamed at the *jawans* and radio operators and soldiers he had felt were responsible, then he had wandered the camp in a daze while soldiers shadowed him. When a *jawan* who had always been kind to him asked him how he felt, he had replied, "I am both the avalanche and what the avalanche smothers." It seemed he had temporarily lost the ability to speak except in metaphors. When the cook took him aside and patted him on the back to console him, and when the fellow who swabbed the floors in the infirmary clucked in sympathy, his rheumy eyes tearing up, Anil told them both that he could finally see life clearly: a heart monitor spiking and dipping — hope and disappointment, hope and disappointment. How life could be reduced to just a wait for a flatline.

His uncle was calling his name, calling him out of his fog, calling him back to Pradeep.

"Why Pradeep?" Uttering the medic's name sapped Anil of his remaining energy. He collapsed back onto his cot, arm shading his eyes from the glare of the single light bulb overhead, from his uncle's concern.

"Come now, that was an accident. Bad weather is only to blame," his uncle said.

"The radio operator never took a request from Sector 10. He never sent a *jawan* with instructions for Pradeep to go to Sector 10. Someone made it up. And now Pradeep's dead," Anil moaned.

"Calm yourself, Anil. You are only making yourself sick. You need rest, not to think about these things." His uncle sipped at the tea but his hands shook.

Anil was unable to stop himself. "They shot Chakravorti in the northwestern sector outside Srinagar to cover their corruption, then got him hooked on morphine to ease his pain. He couldn't stay in the army, but he couldn't leave either. He was in hell. DeSousa had him beaten all those times for revenge, and for sport."

Anil rolled himself into a small ball. His voice was hoarse now. "Isn't it true, Uncle, one should always keep one's enemies close? DeSousa was involved in the Srinagar affair, I looked it up. And you transferred him to Sector 10."

"Yes, as punishment only." His uncle rose up and tried to touch Anil's shoulder, to try to get him to sit. But Anil recoiled and brushed his hand away.

"And were you trying to punish Chakravorti by transferring DeSousa here?"

His uncle mouth opened in surprise, then tightened in outrage. "You don't know what you are talking about. You're just a medical doctor meddling in things you don't have any business to meddle with."

It *was* his business, Anil thought. It was his business that his uncle's helicopter sat on the helipad, but now there was one less helicopter in the hangar. And what had the *jawan* said? Hadn't he suggested Anil ride on the helicopter, too?

Anil forced himself not to cry. He dug his fingernails into his thigh. How he would have loved to put his head on his uncle's chest as he did when he was young. To hear the heartbeat, the very sound of life. He remembered how his uncle's arms were thick and muscular, and that the view from atop his uncle's shoulders made everything look different, exciting. How even his parents had seemed tiny, their ordinary hopes and desires for him small, and easily dismissed. How big he had felt, as if he could conquer the world.

"You are responsible for all of this," Anil said, finally, his voice flat, certain.

"For what? I cannot be expected to remember the names of all the commanding officers, let alone inventory clerks, *jawans* and other lowly staff. How the bloody hell was I to know where DeSousa or Chakravorti would end up?"

Anil doubted his uncle would call for an investigation, doubted even that one, if called, would shed any light on what had happened or bring justice for Pradeep and the helicopter pilot. Nobody would be calling human rights groups like they had done in Kashmir, saying the Indian Army was raping and killing villagers. This was an internal affair. No outside eyes watching. His uncle was safe. Only the men inside, those administering the beatings, the beaten man, and Anil knew what had happened.

The habit of loving his uncle Rahul was hard to break; Anil's love for his uncle had suffused him, this uncle who would have stood at his military funeral and shed tears. Anil led his uncle by the hand to the infirmary; maybe, just maybe, he could make his uncle see what he had done to Chakravorti, what he had done in Kashmir.

In front of the morphine-addled Chakravorti, his uncle again denied his involvement, denied responsibility; he raged at Anil's accusations. "You'll not be stupid enough to spread these lies about, boy?"

And suddenly, Anil could sense his uncle's fear. A glimmer of hope flared. Anil would call the shots now. "Uncle-ji, you have one option now — if you help Chakravorti leave the army with a full pension, then resign, I won't report you."

"Are you bloody crazy, boy?" His uncle's voice thundered, rising in outrage. He advanced on Anil, fists clenched, as if to strike. He stopped a foot away as if he had had a better thought, and smiled thinly. "You think anyone will believe you? They will say you have gone crazy with grief. They will say that there was something going on between you and that medic fellow. Imagine how that will be received, eh, boy? A scandal to rival all scandals!"

Uncle Rahul paused and tapped Anil on his chest. "Here are *your* options. If you continue with your service, I'll get you transferred elsewhere."

"What are the other options?" Anil asked flatly. He wanted out of the army, now, wanted nothing more to do with the army, he would take his skills elsewhere, do good elsewhere. He would let his uncle help him, this one last time.

"Your only other option is to refuse service. You'll be court-martialled and sentenced to our prison for the remainder of your contract, after which you'll be dishonourably discharged."

Anil realized with dismay that he had never understood the rules of engagement with his uncle. Dear uncle, favourite nephew, these were only roles they had played, but these could be quickly tossed aside. He had been hopelessly outmatched, but he had been too arrogant to know it.

Anil saw himself in jail, pacing his cell waiting for the day of release. His uncle would visit him. He would bring English toffees and his wife's samosas, and news of his family, just as if he was visiting a son at his college dormitory. He would ensure that Anil was granted special library privileges and would bring medical journals for him to read so that Anil could keep up. He would even arrange an appointment at the Bone and Joint Hospital in Srinagar to start upon his release. "The Bomb and Blast Hospital, don't you mean?" Anil would reply when told. Since the insurgency, it was what the hospital was called informally; civilians were the main casualties. Nevertheless, Anil would feign gratefulness and thank him. His uncle would reply, "No need for thanks, you are like a son to me."

His uncle coughed, awaiting a reply. "There is no way out of the army, Uncle-ji, is there? I'm trapped, just like Chakravorti." Anil closed his eyes, rocking on his heels. The motion comforted him, but alarmed his uncle.

"Now, *beta,* Chakravorti doesn't have an uncle," he said. His voice was as soft as feathers. "You have your uncle to help you. I am here to look out for you."

Anil sat with his uncle, surrounded by empty cots ready to accept new bodies, watching Chakravorti's breath rise and fall. He was hemmed in between his uncle's solidity and the bunker's metal walls on a tiny ledge thousands and thousands of feet above sea level, and the only way to leave was to jump off.

❧ ONLY CHILD

THE NEW BOY NEXT DOOR CRIES AT NIGHT. THIS IS THE THIRD NIGHT in a row I've heard him since he moved in a few days ago, his sobs filtering through the drywall and mouse droppings of our townhouse. His cry is dewy, like water swallowed by ground, different than the sounds I usually hear waiting for sleep to wax my ears shut.

My exceptional hearing is a Trojan Horse, a curse. The third audiologist my mother brought me to recommended a specialist who exclaimed over my scores, but was at a loss to suggest anything but custom-fitted earplugs. The stoppers, the bungs, didn't really work; the noise still seeped through, sounding like rough wet cloth against my eardrums, but I nodded my head at my mother when she asked, "All better now?"

There were things we couldn't do as a family. A walk in the ravine was a painful experience. I could hear the scavenger birds ripping flesh off a dead squirrel. I could hear the sizzle of red innards steaming. Shopping sprees were kept to a minimum, the hard heels clacking like jackhammers on polished granite floors, the voices exploding like cluster bombs in cavernous spaces, the muzak ricocheting off slick surfaces, leaving me disoriented and dizzy.

It was my father who taught me meditative techniques, how to background sounds, foreground silence. He emboldened me with stories of yogis, of tribal peoples sleeping on beds of nails, walking on hot coals, every inch of flesh pierced with hooks. "All it takes is concentration."

The boy starts up again, little quakes of sound. I'm not sure what to do. Pop my earplugs in? Tap on the wall in Morse code: Are - you

- alright? My father once said, warning me, "There's an expectation of privacy, even if you're only a few feet away." Maybe the boy is simply crying over old and lost things: toys sold at a moving sale, street hockey buddies who haven't yet called him at his new number, hidey-holes he'll no longer have.

In the morning, I wake with a migraine from the tension of being a bystander to pain. I know I have to follow the rules, respect that false wall of privacy, but the least I can do is sit on the steps in front of our house waiting for the new boy to appear, to ascertain his well-being.

I'm doodling an abstract picture of my mother's rose garden, a cubist version of it in blue pencil on the back of my physics notebook, when his front door finally springs open. The boy bounds out, loaded down with a backpack bearing the silk-screened image of chiselled-face Arnold the Terminator. His chubby index finger stabs at the buttons of the digital toy he holds in his hands.

"Hey," I call out to him. "New Boy."

He stops mid-stride and looks at me warily.

"My name's Jay," he says.

If he's sad today, I can't tell. I can see his face, oval, flushed at the cheeks, as if he's raced around the house collecting his things for school. His eyes are huge soft brown orbs, fringed with long spidery lashes. Tufts of reddish brown hair, like my own, stick out from under his Blue Jays baseball cap.

The boy looks like me when I was eight. His parents made him, his kwashiorkor hair, his coppery hue. They made him from his mother's savannah and South African sun, his father's windy heaths and cold English lakes. He could have been my brother, the one my parents never had, but hoped for when buying their minivan.

"Hi Jay. I'm May. Can you draw?" I hold up my sketch so that he can see.

"Yeah." He takes a few mincing steps towards me before stopping, craning his neck to look at my drawings. Then, he pulls out a floppy exercise book and flips to the back pages. Still standing a few feet away, he shows me his pencil sketches, rough diagrams of bullet trains and fighter planes. Every once in a while, a cartoon figure pops out, a beast with a cheery smile.

"That's pretty good for a little kid!" I can't keep the surprise out of my voice.

"They're okay," he says, his head hanging in pleased embarrassment, but he moves closer. "Can I see yours?"

"Aren't you on your way to school?"

"There's time. I'm way early."

"I'll show you my portfolio." I run into the house to retrieve my binder, half expecting he won't be there when I get back outside, but he is, sitting on the salt-eaten, pockmarked concrete steps, tying and retying the white laces of his sneakers. I plop down beside him, but he doesn't jump and flee. I scan his exposed flesh for signs of abuse, telltale discolorations, while he, absorbed, flips through the pages encased in plastic. I even peek at the back of his legs when he squirms on the cold cement steps. I'm relieved that there's no obvious damage.

I've been collecting my art ever since I won a red ribbon in the fourth grade for a sculpture of an emaciated elephant rearing up in a cage, cast in plaster of Paris. In my portfolio there are watercolour renderings of still life, mangoes and papayas swimming in a big boat of a bowl, India ink portraits of my ever-smiling mother and always frowning father and pastel drawings of the street from the perspective of my second floor deck. The latest captured the new boy moving in — the long rectangular top of the moving van parked like a behemoth on our mutual driveway, the tops of human heads scurrying about with boxes. You can see the mother's white line of a part, her raven's wings on each side, the round flat plate of his father's bald spot and the soft denim dome of a boy's baseball cap.

"Is that me?" he exclaims, pointing at the tiny figure pushing a red bike down the driveway to the garage.

"Yeah." I explain the inspiration behind my drawings, my choice of colours, the rationale for each angle and curve.

"Awesome," he says.

My father says, "No man is an island," but the way we live our lives, we might as well be on one.

When we first moved in, our friendly neighbourhood welcome

wagon stuffed our mailbox with dog shit. When that didn't work the neighbours signed a petition demanding we move out and left a copy in an unmarked manila envelope on our doorstep.

My mother was incensed. She marched from house to house, ringing doorbells that never opened doors to her, and then resorted to springing herself at neighbours as they emerged from their lairs. The confrontations always ended badly — shouting matches, veiled threats. Red faced, she never repeated at home what they said to her.

My father laughed it off. "Let them come and try and smoke us out, like they do in Britain. I'll box their ears," his bravado boosted by the boxing trophies lining the shelves in our den.

My mother called human rights organizations, the newspapers. Everyone said, *Things will blow over*. One cane-wielding, grey-locked activist told her, *Outlast them; it's your best revenge*. And it was true. One by one, the neighbours moved out, and one by one they were replaced with the Huangs and Lis, the Singhs and Chatterjees, the Saeeds and Abbass.

But family was another thing altogether.

My mother cried at every one of my birthdays when "ole Grannie" in Belfast never sent a birthday gift but wrote long hectoring letters instead. *What kind of satisfaction could you ever find with a man named Mo-ham-ed Ick-ball Rash-eed, a nothing man from a nothing place nobody has ever heard of?* My father's parents sent a stream of blue aerogram letters from Srinagar with studio pictures of demure, sparkling girls with kohl-rimmed eyes, to tempt and tantalize him. They begged my father to dissolve his marriage, as if my parents' union was only a thing, a lump of sugar that could be melted away with a little hot water and a lot of stirring.

When I was born, my mother bravely tucked a picture of me into an envelope and sent it to them. My Kashmiri grandmother wrote back, "Other Indian-white mixes have produced better looking children with fair skin, chestnut hair, straight noses. How will I find a match for her with her orange skin, her beggar's hair, her pug nose? She looks like nothing, no one."

I'm an only child, in an only, lonely family where no one looks like me.

Despite my offer of friendship, our breezy artist-to-artist exchange, Jay cries again that night, the fourth night in a row. His sobs are penned in, soft horse-like snorts punctuated with a high-pitched wheezing. I march down the stairs in my pajamas to tell my parents about the boy next door, barging in without permission into the dominion of my father, his den, where he sits snug as a ball in a catcher's mitt, deep in the pouch of his recliner, nursing his fifth beer. After ignoring me for a few minutes, he finally gives me a regal wave, an order to sit down. Before I can tell him about Jay, he launches his stories at me. I know them as well as I know every mole and freckle on his face. How his engineering days were spent drinking beer till he puked. How he pestered the girls till they said yes to cheap dates by the lake's edge at twilight. And the one I love best, how, on a dare, he wove naked around helmeted men in a cheering stadium till the security guards finally tackled him at midfield.

"Seize life by the balls," my father says. When he drinks, all the advice he stored up for his unborn son rains upon me.

My mother, scout-like, scurries to and fro, stealing away the brown bottles of beer he's drinking as quickly as he sets them down on the coffee table. They're only half-empty.

"Listen to him at your peril," she hisses at me, before returning to her bunker, the kitchen, to toss the half-empties into the recycling bin.

"Molly," my father shouts. "Get me another beer."

"You've had five already, Mo," she yells back.

This is their Saturday night ritual: skirmishes as foreplay. My father only half-drunk, thinking he's downed more than he has. My mother, disrupting his count, erasing the evidence of his drinking as quickly as it accumulates.

"Molly!" My father yells.

"It's not good for your sperm," she yells back. It's no use telling them about the cries I hear, about the boy in pain next door. They see only each other.

My father is an engineer. During our rolling brownouts, he decides how much juice each community gets. He's a gatekeeper, a dispenser, a god. "It's what most men are in patriarchy," my mother says. My mother is the handmaiden to the god, determined to divert me from a similar fate.

"I could have been an engineer, too, but my studies were inter-rupted by you, my chick-a-dee," my mother chucks my chin and laughs, but I can hear the whine of regret in her voice. When I was in high school, she invaded my room, slipping down from her tiny attic studio and stacking feminist books on top of my doodles, books warning me from subjugating my own desires to those of men.

There in her studio, my mother writes articles for health magazines, magazines she never reads herself, while puffing on cigarette after cigarette. She only reads her slim-as-a-model alumni magazine that arrives once a month, as regular as a period, a lunar cycle, a telephone bill. The alumni magazine is glossy and golden, pleased as punch with itself, bursting with the stories of her contemporaries: their fame, their awards, their wealth. It makes her sullen.

"Don't marry what you want to be," she says to me each month.

When my father gets thirsty he has a place to run to. He revs up the Saab and sidles up to the Indian store where on any given day he can spot someone who resembles him, or his family in Srinagar. He can gaze into their faces, roll his tongue around long-forgotten words, inhale the aromas of ghee sizzling and mustard seeds popping in fry pans, sugar syrup simmering and sweetening in large pots. He can denounce the rise of fundamentalism in India, denigrate the BJP and Congress Party in equal measures, bemoan the violence and militarization of Kasmhir, cheer India's cricket team and exclaim over Pakistan's Imran Khan's prowess at bat, and never have to preface or contextualize his remarks in order to be understood. He can order *chaat papri, Royal Feluda, burfi* and expect that his order will fit him, that no one will question his right to it.

When my mother gets thirsty she can turn on the TV, any channel, and gaze at herself. She can pick up a book and fit neatly into its pages. She can sidle into any four-leaf clover pub and be immediately enveloped into a cheery, beery hug, belting out "Danny Boy." She can slam her palm on the table with the best of them, swearing over the latest betrayal of the IRA or Sinn Féin. She can walk down the street and no CSIS van will stalk her, snapping pictures, wiretapping her phone lines. No one will think her a foreigner, someone to keep tabs on. No one will ever ask her where she comes from.

In order to feel themselves again my parents have to leave each other behind, leave me behind. When we are together, questions fall out of the air like bombs. We are the stone in everyone's ponds, rippling their surfaces, agitating their reflections.

It's why I'm applying to art school in Honolulu, where the majority of the population is like me, mixed. It's my very own Shangri-La, my very own America, the streets paved with gold. I'll have someone else to talk to besides my mother, who has to rush into her library to double-check her responses to my questions in her small collection of articles and books on mixed-race kids, books with sorrowful titles like *Miscegenation Blues, Relative/Outsider, The Sum of Our Parts* and worse. In Honolulu, I won't have to steel myself from absorbing the double takes that are standard fare when our family goes shopping in Indian shops, at Sears and Loblaws, everywhere; the stares that rake my face calculating the degree of genetic transmission attributable to my father, to my mother, as if I was the Frankenstein heir of two different species mating, a praying mantis with a butterfly. In Honolulu I'll find home, companionship, maybe a little love. I'll be able to surf the big wave, riding on its crest, and if I tumble and fall before I reach shore, it won't be because I'm mixed race, but just because I can't damn well surf.

I sit on the steps again, waiting for Jay to appear. *I could make a difference, I could help him,* I think. He's late for school, a little torpedo of a boy shooting out his front door. I wave to him, and he waves back. "Hey," I shout at his back as he races down the long road towards the school, "you want me to teach you to draw sometime?"

He stops abruptly, turns around and grins at me. "Yeah, okay."

Then he races madly towards the school in the distance, towards the avalanche of incessant sound that is the school bell, with a Quasimodo-like glee. For the sake of our artistic relationship, our budding friendship, I have this feeling I'm going to have to background his pain.

On the weekend, my father invites me to take a ride with him alone to our usual Saturday family haunt. We restaurant hop for samosas, Kingfisher beer, and *jalebis* at the Indian strip mall tucked into the desolate industrial park by the highway. There's a video store, a sweet shop, a *chaat* stall, a sari shop, all lined up like colourful little seeds on an otherwise grey necklace.

Each time we go my mother insists on wearing a *salwar kameez* and speaking Hindi while my father insists on speaking English to the pimply-faced adolescent wearing a spiked dog collar serving us samosas. My mother was pregnant with me when they honeymooned in Kashmir. She said she had made a vow to the mountain gods to help me keep my Kashmiri roots. They even fight over my name, my mother insisting on calling me Maysoon, my father using the nationality-erasing diminutive, May. "Everyone uses a diminutive," he says. "It's better than 'Bubbles' or 'Baby.'"

Over a mango lassi and *chaat papri*, my father says he has something to ask me.

"Is it true you are applying to an art school in Honolulu?"

"I love art, Dad." I'm anticipating an argument about my choice of careers, and my arms cross around my chest defensively.

"Engineering is best for your talents, but why do I even bother trying to talk sense into you. You never listen to your parents." He is angry, hurt.

"Dad, you and Mom didn't do what your parents wanted, either," I remind him, gently. "Didn't you do what was considered taboo at that time, marry each other across race? Move to another country? Have me?"

He's not listening to me, sipping noisily. "If you go to art school, you'll just waste your time with boys. At least with engineering, you'll have something to show for it at the end."

It's not a rational argument, and so I ignore him, fussing with my drink.

He tries another tack. "It's just that your mother and I, we don't want you to leave." His eyes are wet, melted water on the surface of an ice rink.

"Dad, I have to leave home sometime," I say, softly.

"Yes, yes, that is true." He waves away my words, concentrating on sipping his mango lassi.

"It's just now, things are different." He sets his plastic cup on the table.

"What's wrong?" I'm starting to feel alarm, a prickling at the back of my neck.

"You are the eldest, now." His twitching mouth tells me he's just bursting to tell me. "You must set a good example."

I can't believe what he's trying to tell me. "Mom, is she …?" I ask.

"Yes. She is." There's that familiar smile, that familiar swell of his chest beneath his gauzy *kurta*.

"Oh no!" It's out before I can stop it, my dismay.

My father stops smiling, injured. "Your mother needs you now," he says, now grim.

My mother's hope is the zeppelin of all hopes. I do not forget to hug her when we get home. She's humming. *Somewhere over the rainbow … there's a land that I heard of …* She's clipping the ends off flower stems in the bouquet my father bought her from the corner store earlier.

My father's elbow prods me in the back.

"Congratulations," I say, on cue.

She hugs me back. "You know this may not work out," she whispers, despite herself. It's a superstitious reflex, something she always says.

"I know. It's okay to hope, Mom."

It's my role to reassure my mother, to stand in front of her, living proof that her body has not always failed her, that conception does not always lead to death.

It's as if pregnancy itself is a drug and my mother's been an addict for over ten years now. There's nothing we can do about it, not my father, not me, just mash our doubts into a little pill and, like my mother with her folic acid tablet, swallow it every day.

That night I hear Jay crying again. But my decision to allow him his privacy, to background the night wet with weeping and foreground the day, isn't working. His pain bores through the drywall to my auditory cortex like a dentist's drill, shrill and insistent. And this time, to make matters worse, I hear words of protestation — "*No. No. Nooo.*"

I throw my covers off and stand by the thin membrane of my wall, laying my hand on its broad surface, as if trying to calm it. It's as close as I can get to Jay. "What's wrong?" I ask him. I whisper my counsel — *run, run, run* — but my breath bounces back, unrequited.

It was in grade school that I started to think of my hearing as a special power. My eardrums shredded with the incessant wailing, whining of children, the chords of their minor and major tragedies. The children laughed at me when I rolled myself into a ball and covered my ears, but I realized that I had something no one else had, like Superman's ability to walk right through walls — a magical power, a super-strength.

If I had a little brother, I would have shared my special powers with him. I would have taught him how to listen for the special sounds that tell you there's danger in the world. Then I would have taught him how to walk through walls, part the molecules of carbon and gypsum so he could escape.

The next day, Saturday, before I can make a decision about what to do, Jay knocks on my door to ask if I can come out to play. My father is in his light weekend mood and laughs heartily at his request.

"His name is Jay. I'm teaching him how to draw," I tell him, darting down the stairs, grabbing my sketchbook by the front hall door, and tucking it under my arm.

"It's a nice hobby," my father concedes, and pats Jay's head.

"We'll go to the park and do sketches of playground equipment. I'm teaching him about negative space, how to see not just the object, but the space around it." I know I sound nervous, fidgety.

"Very interesting," my father says, already distracted by the sounds of my mother upstairs growing a baby in her tummy. "Just don't forget to study for your chemistry exams."

Perched on the wooden risers ringing the playground, while Jay is engrossed in his drawing of the tiny tots play hut, I slip him the question I should have asked him days ago. "Is everything okay at home, Jay?"

"Sure." His hand doesn't even stop scratching charcoal into the thick surface of my heavy bond sketch pad.

"Nobody's sick or anything else?"

"No."

"Are you sure?"

Jay stops mashing his charcoal into the paper. "Is everything okay at your home?" Jay asks me in return, a measured emphasis on each syllable. The question is disingenuous, a counsellor turning the tables on a client asking too many personal questions. He even has the look down pat, penetrating, syrupy-faced concern.

For the first time, I think of what Jay might have heard from his side of the wall. My mother pacing her attic, my father's roaring as he punches the bag in the basement, my own heavy sighs as I sketch furtively, late at night, full of fear at finally telling my parents that I have a dream of my own. What hidden frequencies of meaning could he hear under these ordinary sounds? It makes me not want to pry anymore.

Yet, again in the night, well past his bedtime, I hear Jay crying. I try vainly to distract myself. I peer into the dresser mirror, trying to sketch my face on archival paper, to immortalize its unhappiness. My ears ache. I try to cover them with my duvet, but the sound finds me even there.

My mother catches me crying, wiping my tears with the back of my flannel sheets. She sets her midnight snack, chocolate cookies and a glass of milk for the calcium, on my night table and strokes my forehead.

I don't want to worry her. Anything and everything can cause a miscarriage. I don't have time to think of an explanation, so I blurt out the first thing that comes to my mind. "Mom, my hearing is bothering me again."

My mother's still in her pajamas from the morning, having spent the day frazzled, her head cocked to one side, listening for the footsteps of her muse who'd been tardy in arriving. Her special pen, the thick one with the foam encircling it to prevent tendonitis, still dangles from around her neck. She'd been pacing the house furiously, thinking of ideas for articles, but I know she was in a dream world, a world where baby names pen themselves across blue skies.

"What's wrong, dear? Hearing the leaves bud in the ravine again?"

It's an adult thing, not to believe in special powers, and I let it go, because I know that despite her scepticism, my mother's writing contains an unusual number of auditory metaphors stolen from me.

She sits on my bed, crossing her legs, yoga style, stretching the stiffness out of her back, and yawns, and then immediately apologizes. "Sorry, dear, it's the progesterone making me sleepy." She's aglow with her baby-making expertise, finally making it past go, almost at the end of her first trimester.

"I hear Jay crying." It's out before I can stop myself.

"Oh, that. Well, you see dear, there's nothing wrong with your hearing. I definitely hear him, too."

I'm surprised. If his crying was so audible, then why didn't she say anything? My father, on his way up from shadowboxing in the den, stops by my room. He's not sweaty, but he is breathing hard. He has a potbelly he has to carry with him everywhere he goes.

"I hear him, too. Almost every night. Damn walls are as thin as paper." He shrugs.

I feel sick. They hear Jay crying, but they don't say anything, do anything. "Something's really wrong in that house," I say, my voice shaking with rage.

My father shrugs again, as if saying, *So what?*

This is too much. "If you really had heard him, you'd know he's in so much pain," I say, shouting.

"Now, dear, we can't know why he's crying," my mother says. "He could just have a toothache."

I lose it. "Go, get out. Get out of my room. Both of you." I shoo at them in disgust, but they don't move.

"Darling, you know there's nothing we can do." My mother is suddenly serious. "There's no evidence of abuse."

I stand up and push them out the door, my mother soft like dough under my hands, my father bulky as a sofa, but when my hands touch them, the dry air is charged between us, and they spark at my touch.

We all stand shocked for a second, breathing hard. But I finally hear what my mother is not saying out loud — she, too, is worried about possible abuse. All of a sudden, Jay's crying becomes really real, as if he has just erupted from the shadows, or the deepest recesses of outer space, and landed, plop, in front of us.

When my parents have gone to their guilt-laden sleep, I hear another more troubling sound: someone pacing about restlessly, the stiff fibres of carpet cracking under their heavy weight. Then a bang so loud the walls vibrate. Another bang. Another one again. It could be anything. I've heard sounds like these before, foley sounds they use in movies as stand-ins for a cat thrown against the wall, a child's head banged against the floor, a woman beaten with a stick. But I know it's not special effects.

"Not the boy," I whisper to myself. "Not the boy." It's a prayer, a mantra, the way I used to whisper other things in the dead of night about my mother's ever swelling belly.

I walk over to the wall and put my ear against its papered surface. Silence. Ordinary silence. The sizzle of electricity through wires, the wet whoosh of water through pipes, the brush of undulating sheers over carpet like a woman putting on nylons. This sudden startle of silence heightens my alarm.

My bedroom has a sliding door onto a long balcony that I share with my parent's bedroom. My plan is simple. Jay's house mirrors ours with a similar deck. It's easy to climb over the iron rail and stretch one hand out for its twin, their railing.

Only when I feel the breeze brush the nape of my neck and then swirl around my legs, swallowed in the black gap below, do I question how sensible my plan is. For one thing, I feel a sharp twinge in my shoulder. I suddenly realise I may no longer be able to hold up my body weight. The only way is forward. I jump the gap, blindly reaching, and the railing is there where I need it, cold and rough like dragon scales beneath my hand. I make the mistake of looking down: two floors below me I know is the humpback barbecue, all jagged metal. Straining, I hoist myself and jump into the cage of the balcony.

Like our house, there are two sliding doors that exit to the balcony. The second room is lit up, and I peek in. Through the dusty glass, I can see the mother, stooped over from the edge of the bed tying her white shoes. The father is pacing about. There isn't a single sound coming from the room, just the crunch of the carpet.

Suddenly, the father's arm swings outs and hits Jay's mother on the back of her neck. She almost topples off the bed, but regains her balance and quietly resumes tying her shoes. He hits her again, and she falls off the bed, landing on hands and knees. She gets up, without looking at him, without a sound, and straightens her nurse's shirt, adjusts her plastic identity tag. She walks toward the door, and, before I can cry out to warn her, her husband kicks her at the base of her spine. She dives through empty space to strike the solid door, and bounces off it like a hacky sack, reshaping herself to make room for contact with solidity.

I stand horrified on the balcony until a hand on my forearm startles me. My limbs flail out in fear.

"Shh. Shh."

A small hand covers my mouth. I taste an astringent from soap and something acrid, like sweat. In the fall of light from the room, I see Jay. He has come out of his room to watch this travesty, too. He yanks me into the darkest corner of the balcony just as his father bangs his fist into the bedroom wall. We're huddled together, and I notice Jay's breathing, like my own, is irregular, like a light bulb flickering, fighting for its life.

When his mother has left, pulling herself out of her daze, spilling her damaged body into the envelope of her Mazda, and his father has retreated to nurse his damaged fists in the privacy of the basement den, Jay pulls me into his room. I spot the charcoal box set I've loaned him on his night table. I almost step on his drawings scattered about the floor.

Jay turns up his clock radio. I'm grateful for the cover of sound. There's a psychopath in this house, and I don't want him to find me. All I can think of is my bed, the covers, how stupid I was to leave the soft, coddling cocoon. I'm shivering. It must be the shock, I think.

"You shouldn't be here." Jay's hands are on his hip.

"I heard stuff. I was worried," I say, by way of explanation.

"She's okay, now. He didn't really hurt her much."

Jay stands in front of me, his legs planted wide, his arms now crossed in front of his chest.

"You better leave before my dad finds you."

"Jay, do you want me to tell someone?"

He shoves me and I stumble backwards. For a little guy, he has some strength.

"I want you to get the fuck out of here."

"But ..."

"Leave me alone or I'll kill you." One more shove and I'm on the floor, lying spread-eagled over his drawings and the tracks of a train set. Their jagged metal edges catch in my hair and dangle when I try to sit up. He straddles me and holds me down.

It's our first fight, but not the way I always imagined a fight with a little brother might be. In my fantasies, my brother would have thrown tantrums, screamed, "It's mine," about silly toys. He would have pulled my hair, read my diary, stuck gum in my keyboard. He wouldn't have shoved me down like a cop in a Rodney King video and wielded his arms and fists like batons. He wouldn't have rejected the things I could have taught him.

"Get off of me," I say, trying to keep my voice low.

He doesn't budge. "First promise you won't tell anyone." His clenched fist is aimed at my chin in a threatened punch.

"Fine. I won't tell." I'm bargaining for time, so I have a chance to think. "Now get off me."

He leads me down the stairs, first flushing the toilet in the bathroom to mask our sounds.

On the front porch, I stand in a daze and rub my bruised arm.

He whispers, "I'm sorry."

At first I think about giving him the cold shoulder. But then I feel sorry for him. He just doesn't want his life to change. Who am I to demand it of him anyway?

"Hey, how did you get on the balcony, anyway?" he asks.

When I tell him about my leap, he says, "Cool."

At dawn, I hear telltale sounds. My mother calling out to my father from the toilet. I know she's wiped herself peeing and found blood instead, the beginnings of yet another miscarriage. I hear the braiding of their weeping in the bathroom. I hear the clatter of a phone being picked up, a desperate, useless call to the midwife. I hear my father swear, then storm out of the house to the pharmacy. Did I cause it? I feel bereft, the way I always do after the blood gushes, as if it wasn't just the fetus lost, but me as well, the way I felt last night when I walked into my house and closed the door, shutting Jay out, knowing that Jay, next door, would do the same.

The acceptance letter to the art school in Honolulu arrives the following week with an offer of a full scholarship. In other households, this might have been cause of celebration, but my father, rushing on his way out to do battle with all the other hyper-caffeinated drivers, comes to a complete halt. He clutches his briefcase and squints over my shoulder. When he makes out the letterhead, he snatches the letter from me and crumples it in his hand. My mother gasps, and then begins to weep openly, clinging to my father for support.

"Oh, Mo, why do children always break their parent's hearts," my mother says, clutching her belly.

"Only in this country do children disobey their parents," my father says, stroking her back.

My father turns his accusing eyes on me. "Look, look what you are doing to your mother."

I look down at my toenails instead, but I can't escape the image of my mother doubled over in pain and hiccupping back sobs.

"Are you going to go, then?" my father demands.

"No." It comes out as a whisper.

"What?" my father says. His voice is tight and scratchy with terror.

"No. I said no." I'm truly cowed by the pain I'm causing my parents.

"That's better," my father says.

I know my scholarship is my last chance to run away from the dribbles of tears that fall and splash loud as atom bombs in my mother's cereal, and my father's incessant cursing as he shadowboxes in the basement. It's my last chance to run away from Jay's sorrow, his cries that still seep into my room like a suffocating smog. It's gotten so I can no longer hum a tune in my head, run a comb through my hair, slick polish on my toenails, doodle cheerfully. But I can't make a decision. I'm stuck in that in-between space, one foot forever in my parent's house, the other searching for solid footing, paralyzed by the fear of falling and lying broken on the ground below.

I decide to sleep in the basement. My mother thinks it's because of her heaving sobs. My father thinks it's because I want to sneak boys into the house. I hear the wooden stairs creak as he prowls the house at night, my security guard, my deterrent. The little cube of a room in the basement gets smaller day by day, until one day, I hear my mother scream.

"Call 911," she whispers when I reach her in the backyard by the barbeque. She's bending over Jay, his body splayed, his right leg twisted the wrong way. His lips are a silvery blue and fissured, as if he had lain all night in the desert, all bent and broken.

I race to the phone, punching the numbers for help, my eyes glued on the still form outside, the broken calligraphy of his body. Then there's the shriek of the siren, the glare of the red eye swirling, casting about for someone to blame.

It's not till I read the morning paper at breakfast the next day that the story becomes clear. Somewhere between the inane and tragic, a laser hair removal ad and an obituary for a fallen firefighter dead of lung cancer, lies the news item, compressed into a one-inch by two-inch column in the back pages.

I read it out loud to my parents. According to child abuse investigators, a boy, age nine, had been planning to run away. He had climbed over his balcony in an attempt to jump to the balcony of a neighbour who had once offered help. He fell two stories. Both legs were broken, and he had a severe concussion, but was expected to make a full recovery. He had been made a Crown ward pending the outcome of a Children's Aid investigation.

The news rocks each of us differently. Somehow we manage a breakfast tableau Norman Normal Rockwell would be proud of: my mother at the stove heating up parathas, my father slapping butter onto his toast, me reading the newspaper. But guilt corrodes my parent's hastily constructed shanty of defences. I can see it in the way my mother flicks her hair back and bites her lower lip as she listens to me read, and I can see it in the way my father's hands shake as he stirs the silver spoon into his oolong tea. They are imagining Jay's fall, not the majesty of his flight. But I can imagine Jay, Jay catapulting himself over the edge of his known life with abandon, and I feel a rush of sisterly pride as I witness his spectacular leap. Hidden under the kitchen table my legs bang about, my muscles twitching in response.

❦ THE FLIGHT OF THE PARROT

ON THE SUNDAY OF BULBUL'S HEART ATTACK, MONA HAD BEEN wishing she had taken the time to henna her hair properly to cover the grey. Normally, Mona wouldn't fuss about her grooming, but her twin sister had made her self-conscious not only about her many physical imperfections (her thinness, her buck teeth, her bowed legs), but her single-minded quest for the perfect drought and bug resistant rose.

"When so many people are starving, what use is a pretty-pretty rose?" Bulbul had said to her over the years. Eventually, Mona stopped bothering to explain that most of her experimenting with aromatic plants was for their medicinal values. Then, after a distant uncle, a prominent member of parliament, was blown up in Srinagar, her sister changed tack: "When there is war, why do you indulge in petty pursuits? Looking down that microscope of yours has given you a very narrow vision of the world."

Bulbul's social status, improved by marriage and the coming to power of the BJP, that Hindu nationalist party, apparently gave her the right to judge others. After all, she had been a good Hindu and a good mother, a good wife since she was sixteen. Mona, on the other hand, was merely a spinster with no moral authority. Bulbul, though, had volunteered on every lady's committee imaginable and folded her body in half each day to do puja at the open-air temple near her bungalow across the river Tawi. The trouble in Kashmir had re-invigorated her.

Sometimes, while combing her thinning hair in front of the mirror, Mona argued with an imaginary Bulbul. Her throat ached with frustration each time she told her mirror that the pursuit of the perfect rose is as legitimate a struggle as developing plague resistant wheat or rice. That the two were inextricably connected. That one day while manipulating the gene of a rose she might develop a technique to alleviate the problem of hunger. Though she agreed with Bulbul that science could not solve the problem of war, she resented Bulbul's inferences that what she did was of no value.

Mona had not always been this reluctant to help others. When the mother of Rani, her servant girl, had suddenly died of pneumonia Mona had offered to adopt the girl. But Rani proved inconsolable and had to be returned to her village. Then, Mona had tried to rally around the troubled wife of a colleague at the laboratory whose wooden manner around her young daughter was particularly troubling. She had invited the young family to elaborate dinners at her home, bought windup tin toys from the Ragunath bazaar to cheer the girl, and even lent the family a newborn kitten to fuss over, but nothing she did had any impact on the mother's behavior. Finally, even though she knew she was crossing a line, she offered to adopt the unhappy girl from her unhappy mother. The mother had declined her offer, but rumors about Mona — that she was nothing but an interfering, sexually frustrated old spinster, a *budi mai* — had viciously circulated for a time at the laboratory. Since then, Mona had resolved to keep a safe distance between her and other people's children, no matter how desperate the situation.

"I am a botanist. That is my job, what I do well," Mona said to her mirror in the morning just a few hours before Bulbul's heart attack. "What would you have me do instead? Pick up a gun? I will stick to what I can solve." She had set her comb down with a bang on the cement counter. This time, when Bulbul arrived, trying to seduce her into yet another charitable deed, Mona would be ready.

Silently fuming, she had waited for her sister on her swing on the verandah, staring at the Siliwaks. When she had been young, she had thought of the mountains as a place of magic and marvel, where the twinkling fairies with delicate multi-hued wings lived. When she was older, when her father had abandoned all hopes of arranging a marriage for her, she often thought of how their jagged peaks resembled the sharp thorns on a rose. Since the insurgency had begun, whenever she looked at the mountains she saw in their shapes only hulking soldiers and colossal tanks. And that Sunday afternoon on the verandah, after the phone rang with the news of her sister's heart attack, she saw the mountains flatten, as if dynamite had imploded them; her confrontation with her sister preempted once again.

A few weeks after Bulbul's heart attack, Mona received a call. Her sister had always been headstrong, but even the ladies of the Mahila Association were concerned. "Your sister has been seen running about Ragunath buying supplies," the secretary said. "The refugees can wait. Do see she follows doctor's orders."

Mona, properly alarmed, telephoned her sister right away.

"What are you doing out of your sickbed?" Mona was indignant on behalf of Bulbul's heart, its clogged aortal valves and frightening rhythms.

"Those poor Kashmiri Pandits," Bulbul said, by way of explanation. "Six years in tents before this move to Mishriwallah. Don't think of me, *didi*, just think how terrible it must be for them. They have lost *everything*."

Although Mona read the papers, she had never really thought too much about the refugees. Like the others, she had bemoaned the militarization of the region, the ever-present soldiers in Kevlar vests strutting through the streets or peeking out from behind sandbag enclosures, the convoys of belching trucks endlessly thundering over the Tawi Bridge. She had felt a mild annoyance that she could no longer vacation in Srinagar during the hot months, a mild sadness at the tragic losses of life she read about in the *India Times*. And yes, she had felt the occasional pinprick of fear when it was all too close — a bomb blast at Ragunath or near a police station in Jammu, or on the marble steps of the Summer Parliament in Srinagar where a distant uncle by marriage had gotten himself killed. It was this last event that had increased her determination to keep herself and her sister away from anything political.

"We must do something, *didi*," Bulbul said, pleading.

Mona had never been able to say no to her sister. When she was six, Bulbul had convinced her that they could fly, "*Why else has Mama given me the nightingale's name?"* Mona had followed Bulbul onto the roof, and when her sister had stepped off the ledge, Mona had followed. She was her twin, though not identical, but they did everything together — that was the rule. Her sister had survived with only bruises and contusions, but Mona had broken her left leg.

And now it was the height of the dry season when grass crackled underfoot and Mona's fledgling seedlings at the laboratory and her own rose garden at home needed the most care, and still she could not allow Bulbul to go without her. She agreed to accompany her sister to Mishriwallah, on one condition: that Bulbul promise that the boxes of used clothing, the sacks of rice and lentils, the vials of antibiotics and other medicines, would be dropped off with a minimum of fuss. Mona was to be her sister's living watch, calling out the minutes.

When Mona and her sister arrived at Mishriwallah, a dusty and bumpy twenty-kilometre ride from Jammu, soldiers sauntered out of their wooden hut to stop them at the gate. Despite Mona's entreaties to keep calm, Bulbul immediately took a combative posture, leaning out the window to shake her finger at them. "Why a fence? Are our refugees hens to be cooped up like this?"

The soldier in charge, the one with colourful stripes on his pocket, tugged at his cap and rocked on his heels, but did not say anything. The gun tucked into his hip holster clacked against his belt. He looked down and smiled at the sound it made. Inside the small hut, Mona could see rifles huddling against each other in the corner, as if conspiring about their next kill.

The soldier motioned for his juniors to search the boot of the car. Bulbul was incensed when one pocketed a bottle of antibiotics, but she wisely chose to stay silent. Finally, they were waved through into the dusty compound, where immediately, a group of children swarmed their car, dancing and beating on toy-sized *dhol* drums, blowing into wooden flutes or shaking brass clappers. An open-air music class. The cacophony swelled with such intensity that Mona had to cover her ears.

"A crow's wedding party," the driver complained, but he got out of his seat to open the door in deference to their advanced age.

Bulbul smiled as she stepped out of the car into the throng of children. Mona, following, placed a restraining hand on her shoulder. "This is to be a deposit-and-go exercise," she warned. To Mona's dismay, Bulbul immediately bent to pick up the nearest small child and fling her up into the air.

"What are you thinking? Do you want to suffer another heart attack?" The doctor had been very specific about what Bulbul could do and lifting children had not been on that list. But Bulbul couldn't, or wouldn't, hear Mona above the musical din and the shouts of the children.

"Yellow Auntie! Yellow Lady! Have you any candy?" they yelled, punctuating their questions with bursts of banging and peals of laughter. "Yellow Auntie," they shouted, quite pleased with themselves and their inventive nickname. "Yellow Auntie," they repeated over and over again.

It was not the first time Mona and her sister had been called Yellow Auntie or Yellow Madam for their habit of wearing twin yellow saris — it was, after all, a Kashmiri trait, this habit of giving nicknames. Yellow had been the colour their mother always wore, and thus the colour both adopted shortly after their mother died. Mona expected that Yellow Auntie would be the name they would both be called until their ashes floated on the Ganges. The Ragunath shopkeepers knew this and wouldn't dare suggest any other colour of cloth.

"Yellow Auntie," the children shouted. Mona covered her ears again and looked around for someone in charge to bring a sensible order to this group, for her sister's sake. She could not spot a teacher, but her eye fell on a tiny girl dressed in a red *pheran*, hanging back, partially hidden in the shadow cast by the storage shed. Her stillness, her down-turned mouth, was in sharp contrast to the gleeful children who danced about the car. Her sadness pulled at Mona, but Mona remembered Rani and the other girl she had once tried to help and so she looked away. It was better not to get too attached.

"That's Himal," a stout boy told Mona. "Her father's dead."

Mona wondered how the girl's father had died, hoped it had not been a violent end, but Bulbul was poking her in the ribs with a tin of English toffees, distracting her from her thoughts. Bulbul, she noticed with relief, had put down the child and was occupied with a more sensible task. Mona accepted the tin reluctantly. She didn't want to distribute candies like some politician buying votes. A year ago, a Congress party big shot had distributed saris to the poor; a stampede had been the result, and many children had been trampled to death in the melee.

A hush fell over the children as the sisters removed the lids from the tins with the intention of distributing the candies, two to each child. A little boy of no more than five tapped a steady rhythm on a *dhol* drum as the children lined up to accept their treats. First in line was a thin Sikh boy with his white topknot askew on his head. He handed the cellophane-wrapped toffee to his sister, a little girl with one long braid down her back. Mona had believed, thanks to the propaganda of the newspapers, that after the massacre at Anantang only the Kashmiri Pandits had fled. But here was a Sikh boy, and there, in the middle of the line, clapping two stones against each other in time with the beat of the *dhol* drum, was a Muslim boy, the long white *kameez* of the pious dusty at the hem.

The first set of children walked away, wide-eyed with amazement at the treat in their palms. "Thank you, Auntie," they called back over their shoulders, before inserting the glassy ovals into their mouths to suck. They murmured amongst themselves about the taste, arguing about how long they could suck on the candy before it dissolved completely.

Mona noticed a little boy in shorts at the back of the line, standing on tiptoe and waving his twig of an arm about, trying to get her attention, as children sometimes do in a classroom.

"Yes, *beta*," Mona said, looking at the little boy. The others turned to look at him. They grew silent. They nodded at each other. Then, one small hand after another pushed the little boy down the line till he stood in front of Mona.

"Have you brought medicine?" the boy asked softly, suddenly shy. He was missing his two front teeth and had a slight lisp. "My mother is very sick-sick."

Mona was not sure how to answer and turned to Bulbul for guidance. Bulbul stooped down to the boy's height and ruffled his hair. "Yes, we have brought some medicine," she said, then tapped the boy on his nose.

The children erupted into a rousing chant of "Hip, hip, hurray, for Yellow Aunties." They danced about Mona and Bulbul and clapped the boy loudly on the back, all but the solitary girl in the red *pheran,* who still stood at the edge of the compound. She had not made a single move towards Mona and her bounty, her tin of English toffees. When their eyes met, Mona beckoned with an encouraging, if stiff, smile. But the girl turned and ran away, her tiny fingers tugging nervously at one of the red ribbons in her hair.

Mona wandered about the refugee compound, sent by her sister in search of the runaway child. A flicker of red caught her eye. The girl in the red *pheran* was looping a red satin ribbon through the wire fence that the Indian Army had staked around the perimeter of the camp. A fence that had been ostensibly planted to keep wandering cows, stray dogs and hungry hyenas out but, Mona knew, also conveniently kept the refugees in. The ribbon had been taken from one of the girl's braids, and the freed plait loosened into a soft cape down her back. Next to her, only an arm's length away, a guard sat on a low stool, whittling a neem twig into a pointed nothingness with a large and serrated blade.

It concerned Mona that the guard, his AK-47 standing at attention by his side ready for trouble, cast suspicious glances at the girl, as if something sinister could be divined from a child's red ribbon being twirled about the cold steel wire, as if threat could be found hiding amongst the black fan of the girl's loosened hair, as if betrayal could be read like semaphore in her delicate hand movements.

The girl seemed to sense Mona's presence but did not turn to look at her or stop her strange looping activity. "Where from outside are you coming?" the girl asked. She had the tight, duck-like voice of the very young and an unusual profile, a long and narrow face with a chin that curled up like the prow of a donga.

"Jammu," Mona answered.

Still the girl did not turn to look at Mona. "Can the children outside come to play?" The girl's hands stilled, finally. She leaned her forehead against the wire, staring at the long empty road bordered by endless wild fields, then blinked rapidly, as if something had got caught in her eye — a mosquito, a piece of the Himalayas, a remembrance of things past. As if the desolate view in front of her might vanish and another, more hopeful one, materialize.

The girl's question reminded Mona why she had never before accompanied her sister on these missions of charity the Hindu tea ladies were always concocting to escape the confines of their married lives. Mona had grown to despise charity, an act born of self-serving blindness and poverty of imagination. A rupee to a beggar, rather than an acre of farmable land.

"There are no children nearby," Mona answered, but she found herself standing closer to the girl, as if her very presence could bridge the gap from Jammu to Mishriwallah.

The girl sighed.

Tentatively, Mona patted the girl's head with one hand. Her hair was warm from the afternoon sun. The girl released her grip on the wire and turned to look up at Mona. "Have you seen my parrot?"

"No, I have not," Mona answered. She knelt down, with some difficulty. "Did it fly away?"

The girl shook her head vigorously. Her good braid, clamped off tightly with a neat bow, whipped about, while the other fluffed out into a frizzy mop. Mona resisted a sudden urge to plait the child's hair.

"I'm sure Simi will be very worried about me. Can you go to my house and see if my parrot is there?"

Mona looked down the narrow alleys that passed for streets in the camp, searching for a likely house for the girl, but on each side of the street were identical one-room tenements made of cement blocks.

Again, the girl tugged at Mona's hand, pointing to the mountains in the distance where the refugees came from. "There," she poked her index finger at one grey hump, until Mona followed her gaze. "Can you bring my parrot to me?" she asked again.

Kashmir was off limits. Many of its roads were impassable, either mined or caved in by mortar fire; cities deserted, rubble-strewn. Soldiers and insurgents still bumped explosively against each other in the night.

Bollywood directors had long ago stopped using the picture-perfect pastoral fields, lush *chenar*-filled mountains and lotus-sprinkled lakes as backdrops for their own celluloid explosions.

Mona shook her head. She held out her hand to the girl, hoping to distract her. "Come away now. It's not safe here by the gate. Why don't we go and find the other children?" To Mona's surprise, the girl acquiesced. Her small fingers curled about Mona's palm, like fronds.

"Your ribbon," Mona reminded the girl, pointing at the fence.

"It's for Simi," the girl protested. "So she can find me. But someone has to let her out of her cage, first. She can't find me if she can't get out of the cage, can she?"

Mona was sure the girl's mother would be displeased, the refugees had so few belongings, but she let the matter go.

Together they walked away from the fence and the whittling soldier, who snorted as they passed, and made their way to Bulbul and the other children. Bulbul bounded away from the game of blind man's bluff she had organized in the compound's centre, as if she too were young and not an old lady with a bad heart. She squatted in front of the girl. "Don't you want to play with the other children?" she asked.

But the girl proved single-minded. "My parrot is over there," she said to Bulbul, pointing at the hills again. "Can you get her for me?"

Bulbul looked at Mona for explanation. "Parrot?"

Mona gave a helpless shrug.

Bulbul rocked on her heels and thought for a bit. She stood up. "Don't you worry, *beti*," Bulbul stroked the girl's thin arms, "when next we visit, we will have your little parrot for you."

Mona's mouth gaped open at the absurdity of the promise, but the sweat on Bulbul's upper lip, the manic energy with which she lifted the girl up and threw her into the air, and the girl's squeal of delight as Bulbul caught her on her way down made Mona bite back the angry words that had come to her lips.

Mona wanted desperately to leave the camp. The oppressive heat reflected off the white cement walls, overwhelming her, as did the depressing uniformity of the makeshift homes. She wanted to return to the certainty of her work, the solidity of her pipettes and beakers, the coolness of her cryo lab, and the task of sorting out and cataloguing seeds from rare blooms gathered in Orissa — a task that had a clear purpose and a clear end. And most importantly, Mona wanted to return her ailing sister to Jammu, to the quiet and calm of her bedroom with its cooling clickety-clack fan, but Bulbul was nowhere to be seen and the driver had vanished, leaving the boot still to be emptied of its parcels.

Mona would just have to find a way herself to bring an end to their stay at the camp. She walked over to the car. Thankfully, the boot was open. She tested the weight of the cartons, but they proved too heavy for her. She looked around for help, but the compound had grown eerily quiet, save for the giggles of a small group of younger children huddled in a doorway, and a tall boy counting to fifty while walking around in circles, his head in his hands. A clutch of elderly men were sitting quietly on their haunches watching the children at play.

She tried lifting the sack of rice again, but before she was able to heft them onto the dusty ground, a tall haggard man with impossibly high cheekbones stood up, clucked at a few youths with sparse moustaches darkening their upper lips, and pointed at the car. To her relief, the youths raced to the car and insisted she let them take over the job.

The tall man, a Mr. Jai Pal, president of the Refugee Association, introduced himself to her. Together, they supervised the youths as they lugged the boxes to the storage shed. Mona and Mr. Jai Pal then took over the job of sorting the goods onto the bare shelves, a job Mona found both familiar and comforting.

After a time, the empty shelves were lined neatly with food stuffs, and there were no more boxes to unpack, no more bottles to organize according to type and size. Mona became aware of the silence outside the windowless shed. "Where have the children gone?" she asked Mr. Jai Pal.

"They have most likely returned to the schoolroom." He poked his head out the door and gazed at the empty compound. "Would you like to see what passes for a schoolroom here at the camp?"

Mona followed Mr. Jai Pal and his band of idle youths down an alley, hoping she might spot her sister somewhere along the way, but they were hijacked for tea as they passed by the family home of Mr. Jai Pal. Mrs. Jai Pal, a plump and accommodating woman, immediately served *loon chai* in a porcelain cup with roses printed on its rim. His followers swelled into the one-room cement block home, but it was too small to hold them all. Mr. Jai Pal shooed a few outside, but they hovered near the threshold or peeked their heads through the window.

"This cup you are holding," Mr. Jai Pal said, "is a very-very lucky cup. It has survived everything, *everything* — bombs, mortar shells, a lorry ride, our long stay in a tent that could not keep out the wind or snow and blew all our things about."

Mona put the cup delicately back into its saucer, afraid that she would be the one to destroy the chain of luck with a careless slip. "Please, I couldn't possibly drink out of this cup," she said.

Mr. Jai Pal burst into hearty laughter, slapping his legs with his palms. The crowd at the window giggled and snorted, too.

Mona blushed. She wondered if they were playing a joke on her, wondered if indeed the story of the lucky cup was even true.

"If we are so lucky, why are we here?" Mr. Jai Pal said, his demeanor now serious, waving his hands about the small room. "Why are we confined to this one room, this small camp, dependent on the charity of others, while the rest of the world goes along its ordinary business?"

Mona sipped her tea and tried to think of something appropriate to say, but Mr. Jai Pal didn't wait for an answer.

"In Kashmir, 9,000 homes, 1,600 shops, 1,200 government buildings, 700 schools, 240 bridges, 93 temples, 27 mosques, 2 gurudwaras and even 9 hospitals have been destroyed," he continued, recounting these statistics with a fierce desperation, as if Mona were not a simple botanist, but a reporter with a notepad who could help them leave their one-room tenement, help them return to Kashmir.

Mona had a scientist's brain, and she knew these numbers would remain imprinted on her mind, but she simply did not know what to say to Mr. and Mrs. Jai Pal, who had lost so much. Instead, she rose and said, "I'm sorry, but I must go. My sister has not been feeling well of late."

It had been difficult to extricate herself from Mr. Jai Pal, but somehow she managed, backing out of the small room slowly, nodding in a show of sympathy, while Mr. Jai Pal recited his statistics once again to her. She returned to the camp entrance to find school had been let out and the children were holding hands and skipping in a circle, singing an English nursery rhyme — "London Bridge is Falling Down." Instinctively, she searched for the girl in the red *pheran* but could not find her. Outside the circle, Bulbul knelt on one knee, bouncing a toddler on the other. Mona thought she looked healthier, a pale blush of pink on her cheeks, but Bulbul suddenly placed a hand on her chest, as if trying to catch her breath.

Mona rushed to her side. "Why do you insist on killing yourself?" she said, more harshly than she intended.

"The selfless performance of good deeds is good for your soul," her sister said, defiantly.

Mona could not bear to look at Bulbul anymore. Bulbul's bloated religious fervor, her zeal, irritated her. Mona had a decision to make. She could drag Bulbul away from the camp in Mishriwallah, or she could let Bulbul live her final days as she pleased. After all, wasn't this what Mona herself had been asking of Bulbul for so long: to be allowed to live her life without her sister's judgment? She wondered if Bulbul's manic rush to perform good deeds stemmed from a secret fear that she had not lived a good enough life.

"It is enough, now. You have done enough. We must return," Mona said. To Mona's surprise, and for the first time in her life, Bulbul listened to Mona. She put the toddler down, returning the little girl to the care of her brother, and meekly followed Mona to the car.

As their driver inched towards the closed gate, awaiting the soldier's permission to leave, Mona noticed the girl in the red *pheran* standing beside the guard's hut. As they sped away, Mona turned her head and looked out the back window. Through the grime of the window, she could make out the girl dashing out into the rutted road and breaking into a fast trot behind their car, waving a forlorn goodbye. Mona resisted the urge to wave back, keeping her hands firmly clasped in her lap. The girl had almost made it through the open gates when, to

Mona's relief, a soldier snatched her back.

After depositing Bulbul at her home in the care of her nurse, exhorting her to take her heart pills and lie still, Mona wandered Ragunath, moving slowly from stall to stall. She worried about the shallowness of her sister's breathing, the pale and clammy skin. She worried about her sister's too easy acquiescence to her instructions to keep still, a sign Mona was sure meant Bulbul was really in trouble. She didn't know what she was searching for, but kept looking for it anyway. The shopkeepers presented a whole host of items to her as if they were fragile, newborn babies. In this way, she was lovingly introduced to a heavy iron skillet, a gold-filigreed mango-hued sari, a kilo of almond *burfi*. She nodded at each, and absent-mindedly parted with her rupees, buying goods she did not need or want.

One store finally got her attention. Hanging on the wall was an exquisite tiny paper violin. She remembered how, as a child, she had begged her mother to buy one just like it from a wandering Tibetan merchant who had appeared at their door. The shopkeeper reached for it; he pulled a tiny bow across the strings, and it made a plaintive sound, like a kitten mewling for its mother. She was reminded of the children at the refugee camp banging on their tired instruments. She knew how impractical a gift it would be, that within minutes in the hands of a child it would break, but she bought a few paper violins anyway, to add to the camp's collection of musical instruments. She was surprised by her behavior, for she'd had no intention of returning to Mishriwallah. Perhaps her sister might return there and take the gifts. Then an image of her sister struggling for breath, her hand shaking while clutching a medicine bottle, appeared before her and Mona knew that Bulbul would never make another trip to the camp. She felt faint and staggered against the counter.

The shopkeeper was solicitous. "Madam, are you feeling ill?" He led her to the back room to sit down.

Bulbul was Mona's other half, even if the choices they made distinguished them from one another. What would Mona do when her sister was gone? Who would be the person she herself could not be? Who would comfort the children imprisoned behind fences, the girl in the red *pheran* whose parrot could not be retrieved from Kashmir?

There, in the midst of cartons half-filled with imported toys, an idea presented itself to her. "Do you sell parrots?" she asked the shopkeeper.

He reached for a box on a high shelf behind him. Inside, a small herd of imported plastic giraffes and African elephants roamed about the carton. When she shook her head, he rummaged through other boxes stacked in piles around the room. She could hear him groan and grunt. He placed another box of plastic animals before her. They searched through it together, but they could not find a parrot, only plastic dolls with straw-coloured hair and unblinking blue eyes and "Made in China" stamps.

It occurred to Mona that perhaps a real parrot might be easier to find. It took her several tries; finally, she was told of a potential seller. The jeweller's brother-in-law was looking to sell his wife's parrot before moving to Amritsar. She took a long dusty ride in an auto-rickshaw to the old walled city across the Tawi River, where the man lived in the warren of cobbled streets.

She bought the parrot for three hundred rupees. It squawked in its cage, an old Hindi love song, over and over: "Love in Tokyo."

She opened the screen door quietly to her sister's home so as not to alarm the nurse or disturb her sister. The house was damp and quiet. The parrot didn't make a sound, but when she put its cage down on the side table, it squawked and screeched. Despite the sedatives she had taken, her sister's eyelids fluttered open. "The child will be pleased, *didi*," Bulbul said.

"I will take the parrot to Mishriwallah," Mona declared to her twin. "I will say it is a present from you to the girl."

The return trip to Mishriwalla was as bumpy and dusty as the one the day before. This time Mona had hired a better-humoured cab driver, and the boot was again filled with parcels that rattled and banged about. The parrot screeched at every bump. Mona could hear the old bird flutter its wings underneath the embroidered shawl she had used to cover the cage.

At the gate, a gigantic lorry with a camouflage canvas covering was being unloaded; rice, wheat flour, sugar, the promised allotment for each family. Mr. Jai Pal was supervising three men whose muscles were atrophying with nothing to do. As Mona got out of the cab, Mr. Jai Pal recruited a few more young men, passing by on their way to play cricket in the open fields, to help Mona.

Mr. Jai Pal leaned against Mona's cab and passed a handkerchief over his sweaty face. Mona averted her eyes, hoping to avoid another lengthy lecture on the conditions of the refugees. All she wanted to do was deliver the parrot to the depressed girl and then leave.

"Again, they break their promise!" Mr. Jai Pal declared. "They say they will give us medicines, but our dispensaries are still empty," he said. "The Indian government will not call us refugees, only internal migrants. This way they do not have to allow the United Nations to monitor our situation. This way they do not have to meet certain standards."

Mona thought of the parrot. The cab was sweltering even though she had left the doors open. She reached into the backseat for the birdcage and the cluster of paper violins tied together on a string. The parrot screeched again as she pulled at the cage, then wiggled it out of the cab.

When she turned to face Mr. Jai Pal again, she noticed his mouth had tightened with affront. "I *do* sympathize with your plight, but what can I do?" Mona said, apologetic. She had been rude to turn her back on him when he was speaking.

"I do not mean to burden you with our problems." Mr. Jai Pal made a move to walk away, but was stopped by another screech from the parrot.

"Love in Tokyo," the parrot sang.

Mr. Jai Pal was startled by the bird, as if he was only now noticing it. "We do not need parrots. We need our homes back," he said pointedly, before loping off to help with the sorting of goods.

Mona wandered the streets searching for the girl in the red *pheran*.

A knot of children were kicking a soccer ball about, but they stopped playing to follow after her. They jumped around her and asked if they could pet the bird, but Mona explained that the bird was weary from its journey and likely to bite them out of fear. She handed them, instead, the paper violins. They stroked the thick paper and tweaked the strings.

"Can we play them, Yellow Auntie?"

"Yes, but you must be very careful. They are very fragile and break easily. Don't be too upset if they don't last long."

"Oh no, Yellow Auntie, we won't break them," they assured her with the confidence of the very young.

Mona explained the reason for her visit, and so they led her to a house in row five. With each step deeper into the warren of streets, Mona had felt strangely relieved. The girl emerged from her home as they rounded the corner. She had heard the commotion, heard the bird, and flown out of her home, barefooted. Her mother ran after her, one sandal in her hand, but stopped just as her daughter did, hand on her mouth.

Mona was afraid. There was a peculiar poverty to this act of charity. She had not gone to Kashmir to find Simi, the girl's bird. Instead, she had bought a replacement, an old parrot repeating the lines from an ancient Hindi film song. How could she hope to get away with her deception? Yet, she thought illogically, if one fragile porcelain cup could have arrived intact, surely a bird with wings could have survived.

The girl flung the shawl off the cage, unveiling the bird. She stared, eyes wide with wonder.

"Simi?" It was a question. She looked at Mona, then at her mother, seeking confirmation. How long had it been since she last saw her bird?

Mona could not bring herself to lie, so she smiled instead.

"Simi?" the girl said, poking a thin finger between the bars.

The bird pecked gently at the girl's finger. She looked up at her mother again, her eyebrows arching in question, but her mother was looking at Mona. The girl intercepted the silent exchange between Mona and her mother, her mother's grateful, almost apologetic smile.

The girl frowned, turning back to the cage, where the parrot was fluffing its wings. Her frown deepened, as if deliberating.

"Simi!" the girl suddenly squealed, having made her decision.

❧ THE MOUSER

AHMED WAS A THIRD OR FOURTH COUSIN, THE SON OF MALA LALLA
Auntie, the only auntie we had in Canada. He was an orthodontist, a
manipulator of smiles, he had taken to saying lately with a long face.
He had called my mother in a panic about Mala Lalla.

"Ma is mincing about the house in her girdle talking to the house
mice again."

How he knew this about Mala Lalla Auntie nobody knew, as he was
telephoning from Lisbon, AWOL from his lucrative Toronto practice
in enamels, and had not spoken to his mother in weeks. My father
suspected Ahmed must have installed spy cameras to check on Mala
Lalla, but my father had always been secretive himself, the type to
hide his credit cards in the cracks between the quarter round and the
drywall. My mother had a more likely explanation: that Ahmed had
slipped the maid a few extra dollars to keep tabs on Mala Lalla so
that he could sip caffe lattes and flash smiles in Portuguese at the nice
local lads without guilt. Meanwhile, the expensive smiles of his own
patients sagged, their recalcitrant teeth jostled each other territorially,
and even his ever-faithful receptionist, the one with candy floss hair
and a five o'clock shadow, threatened to file a suit with Employment
Standards for salary arrears.

All this because Ahmed's heart had been broken by his latest
boyfriend, an accountant, who had left Ahmed for a man with fewer
zeroes to his name. Since then, the wired smiles of Ahmed's patients
have only made him sad.

"Why waste time on sadness?" I overheard my mother say to him,
with her usual sensitivity. "No need to let business failures lead to an

undisciplined life. There are plenty of accountants in this world." It was the early nineties, and Ahmed's gay disclosures were still like dog doo-doo to her, something she averted her eyes from while sidestepping. Nevertheless, family was family, and she was busy, so she offered my summer vacation up to Ahmed. "I'll send Sadia, that useless girl, to care for her." My mother had been upset with me ever since I had been caught using her Ziploc bags to distribute packets of weed from my office, the garage, but I think the roots of her disaffection with me ran deeper than even she would admit.

My father tried to mount a feeble protest at her decision to send me away, but my mother had got into her head that Mala Lalla Auntie needed our help. Auntie must have pushed Ahmed away by overindulging in sad memories, my mother rationalized. "What a broken record she is. Partition and Farida, Farida and Partition, always the same two things," she groused. If Mala Lalla continued in her present sorry state, my mother went on, her son would surely evict her from his three-storey townhouse, and then where would Mala Lalla go? Did my father and I really want a dotty old lady living with us? And, just like that, I was conscripted into my mother's project of getting Mala Lalla over the past.

The last time I had visited Mala Lalla, she pinched my cheeks and announced to my parents that I was "a good and beautiful girl." I could use such a pinch now as an antidote to my mother, so I didn't trumpet my protests over being forced to babysit Mala Lalla too loudly. "What about my Mazda?" I said. Holding out for a car for my sixteenth birthday was just something I did out of habit, though I had acquired, as a result of my business acumen, a sizeable deposit on my own account. My parents, son and daughter of shopkeepers in Kashmir, still appreciated a good haggle. Kashmir was a place I'd never been thanks to war — a place people loved to death.

I knew three facts about Mala Lalla's history: that her husband had been the Deputy Minister of Transportation in the Jammu and Kashmir government, that he had been gunned down with an AK-47 on the steps of the summer parliament in Srinagar, and that Ahmed, already in Canada setting up his practice, had sponsored her shortly after. I

knew five personal details about her. She suffered from back pain that
flared up from time to time, made a terrific mango lassi, had once been
diagnosed with clinical depression, preferred that we take our shoes off
at the door. And, unlike my parents, she hadn't rejected Ahmed when
he first came out as gay.

Makeup tests and summer school, second marriages and early parole
for good behaviour, our whole Canadian way of life is predicated on
the second chance. My mother, though, made it clear that I would
only get one chance to redeem myself.

She issued a stream of threats as she drove my father and I down
the green river of the Don Valley Parkway. If I didn't behave at Mala
Lalla Auntie's house I would be shipped off to Twelve Oaks Youth
Detention Camp, and if they didn't take me, to the strictest boarding
school in India, preferably one operated by the Grey Nuns, the same
nuns who had slapped wooden rulers across my mother's face during
her days at convent school.

Multi-tasking as usual, my mother signalled left, then right, and
honked back at drivers she cut off, while delivering her last minute
instructions.

"If you find mice, you set the trap I put in your backpack and get
rid of them, okay? And if Mala starts talking nonsense about Kashmir,
you change the subject."

I made the mistake of rolling my eyes, which she caught in the
rearview mirror. I couldn't quite see myself as either a mouser catching
rodents or a babysitter listening to old lady stories about somewhere
I'd never been.

"The past is past," she said, firmly.

"Tell that to therapists," I challenged, anyway. "Hell, tell that to
geneticists, and the Hindus and the Buddhists."

Instead of scolding me, my mother laughed, a sure sign I had gone
too far. "Your daughter is quite a comedian," she said to my father.
When he didn't respond, she sighed, and her grip on the steering wheel
loosened. "I give up. You win, funny girl." The white lines on my side
of the road disappeared under our tires.

I gripped the armrest. This was a game she often played in the car, usually when she and I were alone, but this time, I wasn't going to be the first to fold. I took a deep breath as the silver van on my right swerved to avoid us. Inside, I could see three blond kids strapped into their car seats, two in the middle row and a toddler in the back, head resting on a teddy bear. Thankfully, they were all asleep.

My mother continued, her hands now firmly back on the steering wheel, "Always this disrespect. Such a bad and terrible girl we have raised, eh Riaz?"

My father seemed to be nodding in agreement, but it was just his head knocking against the side window. Long drives always put him to sleep, too, especially after a heavy meal and six beers.

If the past was really the past for my mother, why was she unable to get over my business dealings? Hadn't I already promised her a million times that I would stop? And what was up with the long row of apple trees she had planted to mimic her ancestral orchard plantation in Shopian?

No, my mother would never relinquish her own past. And worse, she had a permanent death grip on the neck of my own. Nine years earlier at Hillcrest Mall, my bladder bursting from drinking too much soda, I had run into the women's washroom to pee. There were three stalls, and I chose the middle one, the wrong door, according to my mother. Inside, a friendly stranger lurked. He promised me a special gift to explore "down there." I'm sure it hurt, but I don't remember anything, only the bitterness I felt when the police officer with her long blonde ponytail told me I wouldn't be getting my very own Palomino after all. Ever since then, my mother wouldn't let me out of her sight; the furthest I could go by myself was our garage. I was driven everywhere, to track practice, piano lessons, to the homes of my study buddies. Yet now, without any fanfare, my parents were preparing to release me into the relative wilds of downtown Toronto, of Riverdale, the place where criminals, perhaps even the very stranger who had molested me, lurked.

"I always knew you'd turn out bad. You want to be a criminal? Go ahead, be a criminal. Downtown is the perfect place for you. So many druggies there," my mother said.

My mother had no clue; there were plenty enough druggies in

Richmond Hill. I knew because I did a stiff trade in weed and ecstasy without much advertising. When my parents were at home, I pretended to be a normal girl and watched television, reread my favourite passages from *The Hitchhiker's Guide to the Galaxy* and *The Lion, the Witch and the Wardrobe,* and shut my bathroom door to examine my underdeveloped chest in the bathroom mirror for signs of swelling. I really didn't have much else to do but pluck my eyebrows and practise kissing myself in the mirror.

After school, when my parents were still at work, I waited for the doctor to drop by. I had had a crush on him once, his stutter and sad eyes, and the way he covered his dark curls with a bike helmet and then disappeared for hours, only to return bent-backed and soaked as if his very own personal rain cloud had followed him on his long and looping route. But the doctor had been twitchy lately, hounding me to expand my merchandise range to include OxyContin, Percodan and cocaine, and to increase my overall volume of sales. I had balked at the hard drugs. I was his link to the hard-to-reach market, the over-scrutinized South Asian and East Asian kids, but he said I was replaceable, there were plenty more where I came from. So I would get his point, he had pushed me up against the cinder block wall of our three-car garage, waved a small penknife near my face, squeezed my left nipple and threatened to kill me. I managed a hiccup of a laugh at the size of the knife, winced at the squeeze, and even though he lived next door, I egged him to follow through on his threat. But on a cost-benefit analysis, it made sense to close shop and take a vacation. If Mala Lalla was truly as dotty as my mother claimed, I would have a good time in Toronto, and if I played my cards right, Mala Lalla might present an answer to not just the problem of the doctor, but the one of my parents.

Mala Lalla lived in a neighbourhood bordered by Vietnamese grocers, a geriatrics hospital where empty chrome wheelchairs abandoned at the entrance glinted in the sun, and that dark and foreboding medieval castle, the soot-stained Don Jail. As we drove past the stone building, my mother said, "That's where you'll end up if you're not careful." I had heard of the Don Jail, a rendering factory where humans were swallowed whole and then spit out deboned. Ever since I had first started watching late-night movies on television, I felt a strange sympathy with prisoners, not just the conditions in which they were forced to live — their small cages, the baton-wielding prison guards, the brutal gang rapes — but the sad fact that, early in life, they had not been loved enough when it most counted.

My parents found all of downtown Toronto, but especially this area, distasteful: the screeching red streetcars that threw up metallic dust, the streets slippery with vegetables, the escaped criminals they were sure had set their sights on their shiny silver SUV while they searched for a parking space and the elusive green meter. As my parents descended from their vehicle, they frowned in concert. If they could have plugged their ears, held handkerchiefs to their noses, and worn Kevlar vests without looking foolish, they would have.

They didn't see the opportunities — the library on the corner, fat shelves ripe for picking through; the green sloping park overlooking the Don Valley Parkway with its oval gravel track perfect for running practice; the swimming pool, antidote to summer heat nestled amid the trees. And most importantly, they didn't see the unsupervised teenagers walking freely without a suburban van and its requisite parental driver attached to their heels.

Mala Lalla greeted us at the door with a hug and kiss.

She was as pretty as I remembered — her hair still charcoal black though she was older than my mother, her eyes lined with kohl, her figure lithe but full around the bust. She wore a loose *salwar kameez,* but as I hugged her, I could feel the stiffness of the support girdle she wore for her recurring back pain. I noticed the slight grimace with each step she took. Her discomfort, her vulnerability, made me want to offer my assistance, and even my parents seemed to mentally rearrange their busy schedule to accommodate her, similarly moved.

They peeked into the darkness of the house. My father asked, "Any furniture you want moved? Are your pipes leaking? I can get my toolbox. I can fix whatever you need fixed."

My mother fingered the stack of unopened mail, mostly bills, on the console in the hallway awaiting Ahmed's return. She tut-tutted with displeasure. I could hear her thinking: *All those bills, and where exactly is that Ahmed?* Then, consciences appeased, my parents kissed me on my cheek for show before speeding off to their inter-ministerial committees where they lived dangerously, brushing shoulders with deputy ministers who might, one day, get blown up, in the press.

I stood awkwardly for a few moments in the cramped hallway while Mala Lalla looked me up and down and then ordered me to twirl about. "Look at you," she exclaimed. "You've grown even more beautiful since I last saw you!"

I blushed with pleasure. Things were going better than I had hoped. I looked down the narrow hallway to the narrow kitchen leading to the narrow dining and living rooms. Each time I visited, the house seemed to have shrunk. Ours was so large it spread out over the scalped earth of the new subdivision, swallowing hills whole. When we moved in, my mother had been proud of its grand central hallway and high walls. "We'll never find a ladder high enough to reach those ceilings," she had said, and smiled. Mala Lalla's home looked cozy by comparison. I could see myself sitting on her couch looking out the window as the leaves turned orange in the fall, and the winter wind made crystalline patterns on the window. I could see myself sinking deep into the cushions, making myself at home, a home. And even though the walls pressed in on us as we moved past each other in the hallway, I didn't really mind how it forced me to brush up against Mala Lalla's voluptuous softness.

Mala Lalla's kitchen counter was cluttered with stainless steel appliances — mixer, blender, coffee maker, rice cooker — and her stove looked like it had measles, spotted with red drops of tomato sauce. Her floor was slippery with grease. She served me her famous mango lassi in a steel tumbler, and smiled while I slurped my drink.

"Don't you have a maid?" I asked.

"I let her go." Mala Lalla put her index finger to her lip. "Shh. Don't tell anybody."

"Oh." My mother would call Ahmed and ask him to return immediately if she knew about the maid's dismissal. "Do you get lonely here?" I said, to change the subject. I didn't want Ahmed to come back, not just yet.

Mala Lalla laughed, shaking her head. "I don't know what your mother has been telling you, but I'm quite alright here with my books."

I felt disappointed by her response, her supposed self-sufficiency.

"And my friendly visitors," she continued as she took small steps over to the slatted bifold pantry doors and slid them open. "Come say hello." She waved me over to her side.

I could hear the scampering before I saw them. The mice were brown and chased their own tails in the shadow cast by a burlap bag of rice. I shuddered. I could see spatterings of black paint in the corner, then realized they were mouse droppings. What if the mice defecated in the rice? Or scampered over our faces at night? Mala Lalla really needed me after all. If I could make myself useful, perhaps she would allow me to stay past the summer. "I could set a trap," I said.

She shook her head. "They keep me company"

"But I'm here now," I smiled my best smile at her while keeping one eye on the disgusting things in case they came too close. "I'll keep you company."

She laughed. "But you'll be gone before September. And my little friends will still be here." She bent low and clucked at them, as if they were little chicks.

I was trying really hard, but she was making it impossible. "No, really, I'd like to keep you company," I said with more gusto this time. "I could help you clean." I waved my hand around the spotted kitchen.

Her delicate, blue-veined hands fluttered in a dismissive gesture. "I'm sure you won't want to mind your old auntie all day and all night."

"Not true," I protested, but she ignored me.

"I've invited some young friends to take you to the park later. A nice boy and girl who pass by on the way to the swimming pool. In the winter, sometimes they help Ahmed with the snow." She turned to shut the pantry door on her mouse-friends. "Good night, good night," she sang to them.

"It's okay Auntie-ji, I can make my own friends." I was starting to feel a bit exasperated.

"They said they wanted to meet you."

"They're just being polite."

"Nonsense." Her gold bangles tinkled, and slid up and down her thin arms, as she gestured to the front door. "Now go outside and play."

Play? As if I would ever be five years old again. But I placed my hand on the door handle, slipped my feet into my flip-flops. Just as I was about to step outside, I hesitated. I needed to impress on her that I could take good care of her. "Are you sure? What if you need something?"

"What would I need?"

"I don't know," I lied. I looked down at my toes. I wiggled them.

There was a long silence. "I see," she said, finally. She pointed her index finger at her temple like a gun, then twirled it. "Your parents think I'm too sick-in-the-head to take care of myself."

"No," I lied.

"Yes."

"Ahmed's just worried about you," I said.

"Ahmed! So, my son sent you!" She clapped her hands in delight.

"Yes." I clasped my own hands in front of me, like I imagined the good girls do, like I imagined my mother's Grey Nuns did. "And I volunteered to help you because of your back," I lied.

She smiled and stroked my face, "You are so good to your old Auntie."

I was on the stoop of the townhouse, spitting sunflower seed shells into a neat pile, when Ahmed's friends came to call. The tall girl strode ahead of the boy and reached me first, holding out her hand for me to shake, as if we were meeting in a boardroom and I might offer her a job with her very own corner office. "Junia," she said. Her grip was tight and she swung my hand up and down in practised short strokes. She wore her rust-coloured hair in a short Afro, and her athletic gear bore stripes in all the right places. Her eyes were grey and she looked like no one else I had ever seen and I couldn't help staring for a bit until the boy loping behind her came into my field of vision. He was a lanky boy with piercings and purple nail polish on every other fingernail. I stared at him, too. He kissed me enthusiastically on both cheeks and then clasped me to his bosom as if I was a long-lost relative.

Jay prattled on about himself. He lived in the less prestigious low-lying former worker's cottages with his divorced mother, and Junia in one of the tall hill-hugging stone houses surrounding Withrow Park, but despite the hill–valley difference, Jay told me, they had been best friends since kindergarten. "Not much choice," Junia chortled, when I asked how they had managed that feat. "Not too many people like us around," she said. "I'm half-Jamaican, half-Japanese and the girl over there," she pointed to Jay, who winked at me, "is half Indian, and ..."

"Half alien," he interrupted.

They laughed, and then looked at me inquisitively.

"I'm just regular," I said.

I saw a quick amused glance pass between them. I hoped I hadn't offended them.

"Let's make babies together," Jay said, putting his arm over my shoulder. "They'll be so beautiful. Little alien babies."

It was my turn to feel offended. I shrugged his arm off. Were they making fun of me?

"Stop, Jay," Junia said. She turned to me and said, "He's just being funny. Life's just a big joke to him."

I noticed her eyelashes were long and curled prettily. She was more beautiful than the doctor and I wanted Toronto to be my new home, so I forgave Jay and followed them both without question as they took me on a looping tour of their neighbourhood, up and down steep hills.

We were sitting in the park under the shade of a maple tree on the northern slope facing the pool. I sealed our new relationship with an offering of my own special friendship potion, my plastic baggie of hydroponic herb.

"The best time to swim is at midnight," Junia said, licking the cigarette paper closed with her spit.

"Yeah, we climb the fence and then we have the pool all to ourselves," Jay said, refusing a toke.

"Skinny-dipping." Junia said, and then inhaled. She raised her eyebrow, awaiting my response.

Every group of kids has its own test of belonging; I wanted to pass their test. "Skinny-dipping, eh? That's cool. I'm in."

They slapped their palms against my own in a high-five.

"You're alright," Jay said.

"Yeah, you're real bad," Junia said.

"Yeah, you don't know how bad!"

We sat there for a while, Junia and I passing the joint back and forth, until Jay broke the silence.

"Hey, you want to, like, make out?" Jay asked, his cheeks turning red.

Junia smiled at me. "Don't take him seriously. He's still a virgin. "

"Only because I refused your advances," he said, punching Junia in the arm.

I ignored him. Thanks to my molester, I didn't think I qualified any longer as a virgin, but it wasn't something I felt like bragging about. Thankfully, Junia passed me the joint and I didn't have to think about it. I took the last toke, and then we leaned back, the three of us, on the hill overlooking the Don Valley Parkway, and stared at the sky, the trees, the sprawl of our future, and nothing made sense and everything made sense. The short grass tickled our bare backs, and the wind swooped down into the valley and tried to get inside our clothes. The speeding cars, too, were frisky and whizzed by, chasing each others' tails.

Mala Lalla had dropped into her memories, the way fruit flies fall deep into a soda bottle and can't get out, their wings watcrlogged. She was sitting at the mahogany-stained dinner table with a lace doily cascading down its side, slowly turning the pages of a photo album while mumbling to herself. A sodden white lace handkerchief lay on the table. I tiptoed up the stairs to the guest room to hide my stash under the bed. I washed my face free of smoke, and put some drops in to erase the redness in my eyes.

Mala Lalla's voice called out to me. "Is that you, Sadia? Your parents want you to call them."

I made the obligatory phone call from the kitchen. "Are you

behaving yourself?" My father had answered the phone, and though it was only seven at night, his words were slurred.

"Are you?"

He chose to ignore me. "What about mice, is it true?"

I told him that the maid had been right, there were definitely house mice running about, but they were cute.

"Cute?" my mother thundered, coming on to the line.

"Well, not really, but Mala thinks they're cute." I said. "She's not afraid of them."

"Mala is a silly old *budi mai*. We won't have her living like that! Dirty, dirty, dirty! You set trap right away."

I didn't tell them about how Mala had dismissed the maid. "I'm not touching any dead mice. Yuck!"

"I have no time for your belligerence," my mother said, and she would have said more, but I interrupted her.

"Time? Time? You never have time," I challenged her out of habit. "Ma, you are so unreal." I had a giggle fit, then. I could always take my mother's shit better when I was high.

"You think I'm joking? The next plane to Delhi, I tell you. I hope those nuns whip you good, you have brought nothing but trouble on our house. I don't know why the gods have cursed me so." The last was a high-pitched wail.

"Okay, Ma. Okay. Shit! Calm down." Even through my buzz, I had heard it, a troubling new tone from my mother. She was serious. After I hung up the phone, I retrieved the mousetrap from my backpack.

The mousetrap was a carton with printed features to look like a real home. There were even well articulated shingles on the sloped roof. I suppose the mice were supposed to be fooled by the painted gardenias in the flower box on the windowsill, too. Inside, a spring-loaded bar waited to snap a neck, a limb, a backbone. I placed it deep into the pantry, behind the burlap bags, where Mala Lalla wouldn't find it. Mice carried disease, the bubonic plague, didn't they? Or was that rats? Anyway, they were dirty and had to go.

Mala Lalla was still hunched over the photo albums when I walked in. She held out a photo to me. My stomach grumbled with the munchies, but I looked at the picture without complaint. It was a small black and white with scalloped edges, brittle with age. A woman, dark circles under her eyes, held a small baby to her breast. She was surrounded by five other scrawny children wearing Kashmiri dress: embroidered wool caftan-like over-dresses.

"My mother," she said. "When I was three my mother told me, 'you are the thing that was not meant to be.'"

I handed the photo back to her. "That sounds kind of mean."

"Oh, I forgive her. You have to understand, she was almost fifty when she had me, and she was quite anemic from bearing fourteen children."

"That's no excuse." I wasn't in the mood to be sympathetic to parents, especially mothers.

Mala Lalla continued, as if I hadn't spoken. "She was frustrated with childbearing and child-losing and her love was a difficult teat to suck, like dried out sugar cane, and so that's how my sister-in-law became my surrogate mother."

Mala Lalla handed me another photo, a larger one mounted on thicker paper, as if meant to survive mishandling. A stamp on the back identified it from Karodia Photograph Studio, Johannesburg, 1946. I could imagine the photo sandwiched between cardboard surviving the crossings by sea. The photographer had embellished the girl's image with pink smudges on her cheeks.

"Farida." She tapped the picture. "Beautiful girl, don't you think?"

So this was the Farida my mother complained Mala Lalla always talked about. I stared at the photo as Mala Lalla prattled on.

The young Farida sat on an ornate wooden chair with claw feet, her own feet crossed demurely at the ankles. Her hair fell in two long braids, and she had large eyes and lips that curved into a bow. She looked like a mischievous pixie. I liked her immediately. She had to have been brave to come at thirteen years of age all the way to Kashmir from South Africa by steamship for an arranged marriage to Mala Lalla's brother.

"Farida loved to sing. She had nightmares about lions, and this bad habit of pulling at her eyebrows when she was nervous. She knew how to massage feet." Mala Lalla laughed. She held out her foot and mimicked massaging it. "A useful skill in a daughter-in-law. That's how she appeased her unhappy mother-in-law and got what she wanted."

I tried to imagine me at thirteen married off to a whole family, trying desperately to fit in, and having to massage someone's stinky feet. "Yuck!"

"It was a useful skill to have," Mala Lalla said, a smile twitching at the corners of her mouth.

"So what happened to her, to Farida?"

Mala Lalla stared at nothing, her eyes large and vacant. I could feel her slip away again. "People come into our lives and then they vanish," she whispered. "For reasons we have no control over sometimes. And sometimes we will never know what really happened to them. We can only imagine a good end for them, but that is something that only satisfies us for a short while." She folded her hands in her lap.

I thought I knew what she meant. My parents used to receive blue aerogram letters from home, chatty letters about the comings and goings of distant relatives and neighbours, the academic accomplishments of their various children and the rising price of propane fuel. Then as the violence flared, the letters became maps, tracing their flight. "You remember our neighbour Saleema Naz Khan, she has moved her whole family to Delhi, and your old schoolmate Kumar Singh, the government has packed him off in a lorry to a refugee camp at Mishriwallah. That fine jeweller at the market, he has gone to the US to join his family already there." Then, the letters stopped altogether. One of the tragedies of war, my mother used to say, was that there's no one left to tell the news of home.

I supposed the same had happened with Farida; they had simply lost touch in all the dispersal. We sat in silence, then. In my mind, disparate images bumped against each other awkwardly: Farida massaging her mother-in-law's feet, Junia on the park slope, arms folded under her head. I found myself wondering about Junia's breasts, the way her nipples had pointed through the rough fabric of her T-shirt. What would her breasts look like naked? I wondered if they would be soft to my touch, like *gulab jamuns*, or firm, like a rubber ball rolled under my hand.

Before I snuck out for my midnight rendezvous, I checked in on Mala Lalla. Her bedroom door was slightly ajar, and through the opening, I could see her lying flat on the bed, her hands clasped on her stomach, as if she had laid herself out for a coffin. Her head, though, was turned and she gazed at a picture on the bedside table, one of Ahmed in happier times before his father was blown to bits. In the picture Ahmed was a small child feeding a lemur, outside a mosque with gold-tipped minarets.

I pushed the door further open. "Oh Sadia, it's you." Mala Lalla's words were slurred with the painkillers she had taken. She groaned as she tried to sit up.

I walked over and fumbled with the pillows behind her back.

"You know how we lost Farida?" she asked. She motioned for me to sit on her bed.

"No," I said. "But how about you tell me tomorrow, Auntie-ji? I'm really tired." I feigned a yawn. I didn't know if my new friends would wait for me if she started in on another long story.

"Sit." She patted the bed.

It was hard to say no to Mala Lalla, and I wanted her to like me, so I sat, but at the edge of the bed, my feet planted firmly on the floor.

"We were at the mosque," Mala Lalla began, her voice soft, "my mother, my older sisters, me, Farida. We were praying in the women's section, when we heard people screaming outside the high walls. It was shortly after Partition. Men travelled in gangs urging each other to greater and greater feats of depravity: the beheading of old men, the cutting of children's throats, even the slicing off of women's breasts." Mala Lalla made a slicing motion across her chest, and then her hand dropped on to the bed as if it had exhausted itself with the movement.

"Fuck," I said, but Mala Lalla continued with her story, as if she hadn't heard me.

"They crossed this new border that the British had created, the long serpent line, and snatched our women. I suppose our men did the same to their women.

"The screaming had long stopped by the time we dared to peek outside. It was as if the street had performed a striptease; abandoned *chappals* dotted the road, turbans spooled around poles and spilled market sacks, and the *dupattas* — I'll never forget the *dupattas*, they lay like fallen butterflies on the road, their fragile wings crushed. We ran for home as a fast as we could, but the roads were like mazes, and I didn't know my way. Farida was holding my hand. I was so scared. "Don't let go of me," I told her, but somewhere along the way she did. I thought she was behind me, but when we arrived safe at our door, we realized with horror that Farida was missing.

"A year later, after my mother had gone mad and thrown herself into the well, reports started to trickle in from across the border. Farida was alive! In Karachi. In Pakistan. She was the wife — is that the right word? — of a juggler, a man who led a bear in chains into the centre of town and made it dance. There was a little boy now. We, the girls of the family, begged Rizwan to go and save his wife, save what could be his own child, begged our father to do the same.

"I was young and knew nothing of the real dangers of life. All I could think of was the bear, which I imagined was maltreated and kept hungry. 'The bear will eat her,' I cried.

"My father refused. 'She is the wife of that man, now. She has been defiled.' My brother too refused, but was kinder. 'Think of the little boy,' he said to us. 'The juggler is his father and we should not separate them. This too, would not be right. Most likely, she has adjusted to this new situation.' The principal of the local school, even a government minister, tried to persuade my father to change his mind, but it was of no use."

Dread seeped into my consciousness like a fog, the way it seeped into my nightmares. This story would not end well, I thought to myself. Farida would commit suicide, or her new "husband," the juggler, would kill her.

"Later, though much too late, the two governments set up a special commission to try and repatriate the kidnapped women on both sides, but many women refused to return."

"But why?" I couldn't stop myself from asking. "Didn't they want to go back home?"

Mala Lalla shook her head. "Would you return to people who would not have you back? Think of you as defiled, dirty, something to be shunned or pitied? Also, their new husbands, perhaps kindly, perhaps not, stood over them during their interviews."

I pictured a tall turbaned man with a droopy mustache standing over the slight Farida, an index finger to his lips in warning. I heard only half of what Mala Lalla said, how her father had found Farida buried deep in the transcripts of the interviews. How the official record did indeed reveal that she lived with a juggler, and that the child was her new husband's. It had also revealed that she hadn't wanted to return to India. She had made a request, though, that had been duly recorded in the transcript. '*Although I do not want to leave my son permanently, could I be sent to South Africa to visit with my parents?*' On the yellowing paper there was a notation that the matter was referred to the Deputy Minister, but there had been no information as to the outcome.

"Farida, so scared of the lions, had come all the way from the savannahs, the veldts, for a suitable match, only to find that lions were everywhere. Still, she survived. She made a life for herself in her new home." Mala Lalla sighed.

"But her life sucked, she was kidnapped, she was raped," I said. "And nobody cared." I was angry; Mala Lalla didn't seem to get it.

Mala Lalla nodded, as if she was just now considering my point of view. "This is true, nobody really cared about Farida."

I wanted to leave Mala Lalla then, to just leave the world of adults and go play with Jay and Junia. Why did she have to tell me this story, anyway? What was I supposed to do with it?

"Why do we make it impossible for people to come home again?" Mala Lalla said, starting to sob.

I heard my mother's voice in my ear urging me to tell Mala Lalla to get over it, to not dwell on the past, but I couldn't bring myself to repeat my mother's harsh words. I could see the Grey Nuns swishing as they walked in a circle in a courtyard, fingering their rosary beads and praying for patience to deal with the delinquent Canadian girl that had been foisted upon them. But I put my hand over Mala Lalla's hand and let her cry, anyway. And then it dawned on me, "Ahmed will come home again, you'll see," I reassured her.

Still, maybe my mother was right, maybe indulging in memories was a dangerous thing, like shooting a gun off at the Line of Control.

When my mother heard news that her ancestral village was bombed out, nothing but rubble and ruin, it had taken a trip to the psychiatrist and four months on her government short-term disability plan for my mother to snap herself out of it. The psychiatrist had forced her to count backwards from 100 in intervals of sevens. "There's nothing wrong with my brain," she had protested, "I'm grieving." But she filled the prescription for antidepressants the doctor had given her anyway. Then she declared herself cured. Her trick: "I just won't think about it, anymore. Chapter closed!"

I continued patting Mala Lalla's hand till she turned onto her side and sighed deeply. I could see that it would be a candy-striper kind of night. Mala Lalla's legs were spidery thin, and when I lifted her to slip her under the sheets, her body was light as a pillow. It made me want to comb her hair, fuss about the pillows again, and hold her hand while she drifted off to sleep.

Just as I was shutting the door to her room, Mala Lalla called out to me. "If Ahmed calls, tell him to come home, tell him I'm sorry." And I could see that she really was.

Junia and Jay were not by the third lamppost near the park bench with the missing slats. I went in search of them at the pool, stepping with some trepidation in and out of the little falls of light cast by the streetlamps. Would they be angry with me for being late? Think I was chicken? The tall fence proved not too difficult an obstacle, my toes finding a grip in its diamond mesh pattern. They were sitting on the diving board, whispering to each other. I approached them, sniffing the water for over-chlorination, but Jay was a lifeguard, so he knew the lifeguard's routine.

"Don't worry, the water's safe. It won't burn you or gas you to death," Jay laughed.

I sat on the edge of the deep end, my lower legs dangling in the water. Jay stripped off his cargo shorts, but turned modestly away from us to dive in. I saw the smile of his crack just before the spray of water hid him in its indigo depths. Embarrassed, I turned to look at Junia who was tugging her purple sports bra over her head.

"Second thoughts?" she said. She slipped her soccer shorts off to reveal her ivory-coloured pelvis, a shock of black hair in a V shape.

"What if someone comes?" I whispered. I looked up at two slabs of white, buildings that stood erect in the darkness of trees, rows of windows facing us. "Or what if they're hiding in the shadows taking pictures?" I had an urge to run away.

"Come on, we'll go in together." She held her hand out to me. She was standing nude in the dim light, her crotch at my eye level. Jay was watching us, submerged up to his eyes, like a crocodile in a swamp.

He lifted his head out of water. "I wish I had a camera, right now," he said.

I grabbed Junia's hand so she could pull me up. She leaned close, and I could feel the tips of her nipples brush my own through my tank top. She giggled. "I've got goose bumps."

I took a step back and rubbed my hands up and down her arms to warm her.

"Thanks," she said. Then she pulled me towards her again; at first, I thought she meant to kiss me, but she yanked my shorts down so they fell to my ankles. Half unpeeled, I stripped off my T-shirt and turned away from her, slicing the water in half to hide.

Later, after the requisite dunking and splashing and underwater grabbing of ankles, Jay brushed up against me, pinning me to the slimy tiled wall of the pool, but somehow keeping his lower half, his dangling penis that looked like a big minnow, away from me. I couldn't look him in the eye, and I thrashed about till Junia swam up to us.

"Off, Jay." She pulled him away from me.

Jay dog-paddled away, whining and howling, pretending to be a dog in heat. It made me sick, how scared I had been when Jay pushed against me.

I pulled Junia towards me, but I hadn't anticipated how hemmed in I would still feel, as if I was trapped in a small room with a door just out of my reach. I moved away, deliberately knocking Junia's foot out from under her, and she resurfaced coughing.

"Sorry," I said.

"Are you crazy?" she said.

I really was sorry. "I'm sorry. I'm sorry!"

She swam away, but then turned towards me and nodded, but she kept her distance, one hand clutching at the pool's edge.

I thought a bit about how the past could be the past. I pushed through the water till I was finally by her side.

"I like you," I said.

We must have been really stoned to do what we were doing under Mala Lalla's dogwood tree. I was sandwiched between a writhing Junia and a gyrating Jay, while the crickets chirped and the cicadas sang. Someone's hand was on my right breast, and someone else's hand was squeezing my bum. Was it Jay's or Junia's? Who cared? It felt good. My own hand was travelling down a smooth abdomen to the abyss, the rim, the ridge of fabric encircling a tiny waist, and what I might find when I plunged down mattered less to me than getting there. We were travellers on a crowded bus, bumping up against one another with good-natured affection. The weed had us smouldering. Our eyes were closed; tomorrow we wouldn't know who had done what to whom. It was this last fact, our deliberate hoodedness, which allowed Mala Lalla to open the kitchen slider, cross the wooden deck in her slippered feet and plant herself a few feet away without us noticing.

"Sadia. What's going on here?"

I kept my eyes closed. Only Junia and Jay were here with me on this journey. Everyone else was far away, far in the distance, and I wanted to keep it that way. But, a hand was snatched back from my buttocks, and I felt a body spring away from me.

It was Junia, escaping. "I think it's time for us to go home." She grabbed Jay's arm and pulled him from behind me, revealing him to Mala Lalla as if he were a small boy hiding behind a tree or the skirt of his mother.

"Hey, it's nothing," Jay said to Mala Lalla, shrugging. "Nothing serious."

He thought he needed to calm her down, but I could see she wasn't angry. She was shaking her head. Overhead, there was a small halogen porch light, and I could see her eyes brimming with tears. Too many sad people in the world, I thought, too fucking many.

As I walked up the stairs to the guest room, I heard the scrape of a door. Mala Lalla at the pantry talking to her mice again, no doubt, before falling on the bed and into a deep sleep.

It must have been the weed. I had my recurring dream, a dream that I've had since the man in the washroom; a pack of wild Dobermans chased me down a narrow hallway lined with doors. But I wasn't alone this time. A girl in a *pheran* ran beside me. Somehow, I knew it was Farida. We had only seconds to choose. What if the door we tried was locked? Farida opened one door and raced through it, but I hesitated, crazy with indecision. Which door, really, would be the one to safety?

I woke up trembling from my nightmare. And then I remembered Mala Lalla's shocked face at the sight of me and Junia and Jay under her dogwood tree. Her hands had been cold and clammy on my back as she had pushed me up the back steps and into the house. Would she kick me out, call my parents? The doctor would be the least of my problems if Mala Lalla told them I had been caught heavy petting with not just a boy, but a girl, too.

I knew how my parents felt about Ahmed. Indeed, my vocabulary had swelled considerably after my parents spotted Ahmed with the mayor of Toronto on the front page of the *Toronto Star*, bare-assed in leather chaps, his right hand on the bare bum of another man, riding a glittering truck in the Gay Pride Parade. Ahmed's boyfriend, the accountant, had been angry about the picture, too, and shortly afterwards he had left Ahmed. Mala Lalla had been angry about that picture also, not the nakedness, or the front page business, but about the other man, the man not the accountant.

In the end, I didn't have to worry about Mala Lalla telling my parents about my sexual sortie. Early that morning, I heard a scream and rushed down the stairs in my T-shirt and underwear to see what was wrong. The LED lights of the microwave flashed their belligerent news. It was only 5 a.m. Mala Lalla was leaning against the frame of the pantry, clutching a teapot, her mouth agape, one hand pressed against her heart. Was she having a coronary?

"My little friend," Mala Lalla cried. She pulled away from the doorframe as if it had been hotwired. A sob came ripping out of her body. She looked at me accusingly. "This was her home!"

"Oh, God," I said. I had forgotten to check on the mousetrap, too stoned, too busy thinking only of myself.

I pushed past Mala Lalla to see if I could somehow undo the damage I had caused. In the dim light I could see a tiny brown mouse. Its body lay half outside the trap, its lower legs caught in the pincers. A darkness had stained the carton where the body lay, still struggling. When I tried to pick it up, Mala Lalla became even more hysterical.

"How could you do this?" she said, her voice rising.

I tried to apologize, but she was inconsolable.

"You killed my friend! How could you be so wicked," Mala Lalla screamed over and over again, her finger wagging in my face.

It was just a mouse, I wanted to say, but my legs felt wobbly. I sat down and put my head down on the sticky table, trying to block out Mala Lalla. Jay and Junia would be at home sleeping peacefully in their beds. Nobody was accusing them of murder at five o'clock in the morning. It was all so unfair. I raised my head and stared at Mala Lalla, still standing there with her finger pointing at me. I rose from my chair with, I swear, the purest of intentions. I just wanted everyone who had ever called me wicked, bad, or dirty to just stop.

"Mala Lalla Auntie get over it!" I yelled. God, if I could force myself to get over my stuff, why couldn't she?

But as soon as my words were out, I regretted them. Mala Lalla went silent, so silent I thought I could hear the whooshing of electricity through the wires in the house. She glared at me, this woman who had pinched my cheeks with affection, who had made me mango lassi, who had told me about the plucky Farida, who had taken me in when my parents had turned against me.

She glared at me as I dialled my parent's number, and she continued to glare at me as I begged my parents to return me home. I didn't want to leave Mala Lalla, but I knew she would never be able to stand the sight of me again.

❧ In the House of Broken Things

My Canadian visitors are perched awkwardly on my rickety dining room chairs, ready to spring up and offer me help with the tea tray, but for my protestations. It's the sloshing of tea over the rims, the dangerous tilt to the tray that has them alarmed. They assume old age is responsible, but in truth my shakes are from the trouble I've had lately. Theirs was an unexpected courtesy visit, full of awkward moments and stiff smiles and gifts from North America my cook would appreciate: the requisite blender, griddle and kettle, a hair dryer, and a special adapter to make it all work right.

The man, Mohammed, was my charge a long time ago, long before my hair turned grey, so long ago I have almost forgotten him, almost forgotten myself, the woman in an orange georgette sari with dangerous songs of freedom in her head. When I was that woman, he was a bespectacled young man in an imported tweed blazer and white cotton pants on his way to study electrical engineering in America, his wife, the Irish prize he first brought home to Srinagar and married in a traditional wedding *zari*.

My guests have brought other gifts. They slide their daughter towards me across the rosewood table. It is a sunny photograph, the girl wearing too-tight shorts and leaning against a surfboard staked in the sand, an expanse of ocean behind her. Her hair is wet and stringy, her legs slick and glossy. I can almost smell the coconut oil on her skin. There's no car in the picture, but later in the evening she will drive down a coastal highway, her long hair blowing back in the breeze, singing off-key to the radio.

"Times have changed," my old charge says, apologetically. He thinks his daughter's bare legs and exposed cleavage scandalize me. He doesn't know that I am relieved by the image, by what I don't see on that beach — soldiers and barbed wire and sandbags — the girl, a wingless starling, her limbs amputated by a mine. Or the girl, an upturned lotus floating face down at Dal Lake, her sari twisted around her like a noose.

"She's away at university studying art. She's always had a mind of her own." My guests babble on about their daughter, the first sculptures she made out of soap bars at six, tin cans at eight, but I am no longer listening. I am thinking of the girl in the photograph, the ocean that looms behind her. I am thinking of all our oceans, the way we grasp at the shore, leaving long trailing grooves in the wet sand when pulled back to sea, when forced to let go; how even in the natural world desperation exists.

I force myself to return to the conversation. They had in mind a trip to his ancestral village near Srinagar, my guests are explaining, but the Canadian Consulate in Delhi has dissuaded them. "We were told Kashmir is in lockdown," the wife says. She is a nervous woman, twisting the handle of her purse this way and that way.

"We are very disappointed, naturally, but we have nobody to blame but ourselves," my old charge says. "We should have known the ceasefire wouldn't last. It was in a moment of madness that we bought the tickets. Homesickness, nostalgia, you know." He shrugs.

"Home is never what you remember, anyways," his wife says, patting his knee.

"We've just done Ireland, my wife's country, too." He squeezes her hand.

"What will you do, then?" I ask my old charge, curious. I wonder what sort of man he has now become.

The wife rushes to answer. "A visit to the Taj Mahal. Some other day trips, too, I imagine, though he doesn't much like doing touristy things."

I notice a strange look pass between them. The usual tension between couples, I imagine.

"Then, we're off to Goa and the beaches. I don't mind a bit of sun." Her chirpiness is now forced. She puts a hand on her belly, as if communing with her insides.

My old charge notices her gesture, but before I can muster the expected clucks and coos over the good news, he catapults himself from his chair. "We'll come to see you again just before we leave. Thank you for your help," the husband says. "If there's anything I can do to repay your kindness so many years ago ..." He glances about my flat, as if just now noticing the broken things that lie where they were damaged: my divan with its coir stuffing hanging out like a hernia; my side table, rickety on three legs, the fourth hacked by a scimitar; my dining room chairs nicked and wobbly and my vase half glued back together from dust, large fragments of which still crunched under my *chappals* as I wandered my flat. I had not had the time to shop for replacements. I should have swept the floor again.

"It was my duty to help you," I say, simultaneously embarrassed by his thanks and the state of my house.

"How have you been keeping?" the husband asks, a spot of worry in his voice.

I rub my stiff knees beneath my sari, and point at my eyes greying with cataracts, then shrug.

He nods in understanding. He, too, is growing old. He shakes his head sadly.

"We think if we are far away that we are not affected," I say changing the subject. "But the trouble always follows us, whether we are indifferent or involved." I was thinking not of him, but myself, but by his puzzled look I knew he had not understood.

There is a story I need to tell him about myself, to remind him about his old home, about the terrible revelations of telegrams and trains. He has been away too long, he has forgotten.

Each season a new child appears on my doorstep, and each season I must sweep aside my plan to vacation by the seaside in Madras with my sister.

Sometimes I am forewarned. A telegram arrives, marked with watery rings from chai-sipping clerks at the telegram office, the sweat-stained thumbprints of the asthmatic bicycle courier, the charred burn holes from my *bidi*-smoking gatekeeper who holds the envelope to the light in an attempt to discern its contents.

"From your people in Kashmir?" The gatekeeper mops his bald spot with a frayed handkerchief. He pecks for a response so that he can justify a few minutes of absence from his post. His is a forlorn hope that I will save his balding head from the blistering sun that reflects off the whitewashed concrete of the towering buildings, that stuns him into a stupor by midday. I do not like this man. I send him on his way with a shrug.

The ink on the telegram is from an exhausted typewriter ribbon nobody has bothered to change, already fading, making it difficult to read without glasses. Urgency is always evident, spelled out not in any words one might look up in a dictionary, but in the gaps.

Nampreet, son of Jatinder Singh from Poonch arrives 6:20 p.m. by train. Please find job. Money follows soon.

Amina Chand, daughter of Satish Chand of Jammu arrives 5:40 a.m. seeking assistance with job.

Faizal Khan, son of Rizwan Khan of Srinagar arrives at 4:30 p.m. seeking scholarship abroad.

Sometimes the children arrive without warning, and the gatekeeper escorts them to my apartment, rapping hard on my door with his heavy cane stick.

"This one better not bring trouble," he warns.

They come carrying bundles, old bedclothes hastily stuffed and lumpy with impractical nostalgia — the protruding hip of a picture frame, the medals clanking against one another, the rolls of canisters containing their college diplomas or favourite poster of Shabana Azmi. They come, their mother's pain, their family's sacrifice spreading out behind them like a shadow, following them wherever they go. They sit at the edge of the cot in my spare room, more exhausted by the heavy weight of rushed kisses and weepy goodbyes than by the rigor of the ear-popping descent down the mountain, the hard seats and jolting bus ride, the frostiness of unheated train interiors.

I am the mother of each child, the conductor to their future, their chaperone to life. I make no distinction between boy and girl, between

Muslim and Hindu, Sikh and Buddhist, village or town. My mother was Hindu, my father converted to Sikhism, my sister eloped with a Muslim fellow in college in Madras. Myself, I am a teacher, and the only obeisance I condone is to the god of education, to scholarship.

Two of my charges have received scholarships abroad and never returned. Three have gone on to teach at girls' or boys' colleges across India. Four have found employment in Bangalore's Silicon Valley as customer service representatives, trained in computers and American style politeness, their tongues ironed flat to Americanisms. Some have repaid me many times over, and I use the sums to attend to my next charges.

It is this very success and my presumed stash of money (sewn into my mattress, stuffed into my vases, taped to the underside of my table) that has resulted in this most recent violation of my home. I suspected the gatekeeper, known to spread rumors at choleraic speed. It is his rumours, I am sure, that has caused the waving of scimitars, the threat of petrol bombs, the hissing suggestion from one side or another that I am a sympathizer.

I notice my old charge is frowning. He taps his foot on the ground, and pulls at the fabric of his pants at his crotch. He wants to interrupt and ask questions, but I continue with my story. I have barely begun.

The last attack came six nights ago. I was alone, asleep in my bed, the mosquito net wafting in the breeze of the overhead fan. I could hear their footsteps, loud and belligerent, in the tiled corridor. They hesitated at the door.

"Yar, make bloody sure this is the right one."

"Number 40, this is it."

Then the shudder of the door as they rushed it with their shoulders, the soles of their feet. The bolt held only a few minutes before the pins flew this way and that way in response to the heft of an axe.

There was the obligatory waving of the scimitar around my head, the obligatory swearing and spitting, the half-heartedness of their attempts due as much to the advanced state of their intoxication as to the realization of my advanced age. They had been expecting someone half my age. Brutalizing an old woman was not half as fun as kicking young men around in the Sikh quarter, or pouring gasoline on a Muslim, stoning a Hindu.

Yes, I could tell you what religion they belonged to, for each person comes into this earth shackled by a legacy, a heritage, a culture, a religion. Some renounce their past, some embrace it, some walk many steps away from it the better to cast a critical eye at it. These three, their gaze fell critically only on other people's religion. I could smell the blood of men on their *kurta* pajamas, on their polyester pants and nylon shirts. From experience, from trains that arrived bleeding during Partition, I can tell you that bloodlust stinks the same on every side.

What they did to me, I will not tell you. Suffice to say, I fell unconscious. I was not much fun.

My old charge springs up to fuss over me, as if the attack had just happened. There is outrage in his voice, outrage at what was done to me. The wife stands up and offers to get me a glass of water, but she does not know her way to the kitchen. I wave at them both to sit down. My old charge refuses, and paces the room as I resume speaking.

My attackers left after ransacking my place, after finding the sought after treasure, a tight wad of rupees hid in the strongbox of a biscuit tin. This of course was not the sum total of my wealth. I have always deposited my money into several banks scattered about Delhi. What they stole was the money I had saved to buy a ticket to visit my sister in Madras. I had in mind for us a small seaside vacation, a rest from the bad smells of Delhi, its diesel fumes, the two-storey-high mounds of refuse on the side roads, the toxic tang of chemicals brewing in industry.

I wish I could say the attack did not affect me, but it did. I became suspicious of everyone, my neighbours, the gatekeeper, of men smoking cigarettes or *bidis* passing by outside my balcony window. These three strangers had researched me before staging their visit, I thought. Someone must have passed on their inaccurate information about me. Luckily this brief state of paranoia did not last.

I could no longer afford a train ticket to Madras and my vacation

by the sea; my sister would be disappointed, but not surprised. I tried to satisfy myself with thoughts of wandering the Delhi streets in search of a new divan, but I found I could not step outside my apartment. It was as if an ocean had surrounded me, and a strong current was pulling me away from the door. Then, the next telegram came. I embraced it in defiance and slammed the door on the gatekeeper who waved his cane in my face. "I cannot protect you if you continue to bring trouble into my compound."

The new divan would have to wait for better times. I was tired of the frightened old woman I had become since the attack. Where was that woman in the georgette sari with songs of freedom in her head? Had I not marched against the British, written articles for the newspaper about the failure of the promise that was Independence, argued over chai with many a wild-haired man who could quote Marx and Engels but would not speak up for women's equality? Did I not forfeit my job as principal rather than deny my convictions when parents complained I was putting crazy ideas into their daughter's heads and making them unmarriageable? I would not now be made to cower at the feet of ignorant men!

A girl from Srinagar will be arriving shortly. The army ransacked her mother's home looking for insurgents. Cots, pots and pans, tables and chairs, an ancient rosewood *almirah*, all kicked outside, doused with kerosene and set alight. How then can my feet not walk to the train station, and I, gazing upon her fearful countenance, not reach out to her, speak her name and welcome her into my home? How many like her have I raised, young girls and boys from Kashmir, fleeing their prescribed fate?

As I pause to gather my thoughts, to catch my breath, my guests take the opportunity to speak. They still don't understand. "After all that has happened, why put yourself at more risk?" they ask.

I tell them another long rambling story about one of my charges, a young Marxist with a PhD from Oxford and little common sense. He had sent me a long letter complaining of his ill wife, his rude children, the grey English skies, describing his longing for one more glimpse of Srinagar Lakes clogged with lily pads, lotus leaves. He wrote, "Why did you help me?" I wrote back, "I would give all my life to those who need it."

The truth, though, is always more personal. My sister's son, Krishen, bound for home after his university exams, was caught up in the inexorable net of the Bombay Hindu-Muslim riots of 1985. I think now with regret of how we had coached him. How a little lie might have saved his life.

Walking by the sea wall munching on peppery *channa* in newspaper cones, we would tease, "Koo-Koo, are you Hindu or Muslim?" just to hear his response. "If I am not the one, then I am the other," he would say like a sage, flashing the mischievous smile of his Hindu mother at us, then ripping forth with the irrepressible laughter of his Muslim father before running off to join his cousins skipping stones across the impervious surface of the sea. And what was his end for all our coaching? During the riot, when asked to declare himself, "Are you Hindu or Muslim?" he refused to do so. He was pulled off the train, his hands cut off before the fatal blow to his head with a brick.

All stories must stop somewhere, after all, so I ended mine here for the sake of my guests and perhaps, if I am honest, for myself. The details of my grief, they did not need to know; the details of my grief, I did not need to relive.

I show my guests my train schedule, with its endless columns of departure and arrival times, and ask them, if they are still in Delhi, to escort me to the station in three day's time. I am, after all, an old woman, frail and still afraid. I am old enough to acknowledge this fear: fear of the obstreperous gatekeepers, fear of the trains that arrive bleeding, fear of the men waving about axes that hack at the innocence of others. "You can help me, by taking me to the train station and waiting with me for my new charge," I tell them. "But, I warn you, we may be followed."

"But why would you do this, take these risks, after all that has happened?" my old charge asks again. He wants to be like the surface of the sea, impervious to skipping stones. It is not that he is indifferent, just afraid.

I tell them it is for Koo-Koo that I will accept this new girl from

Srinagar into my home. She will arrive and I will usher her into my dishevelled parlour. She will look around at the plunder, my ripped divan, my legless table, the smashed crockery. And she will say, "Here, too?" It will frighten her, but it will not be new to her, the litter of broken things strewn about our home.

My guests are shifting in their seats, in turmoil. They have not crossed oceans to take on the misery of others, but to vacation, to reminisce in peace, the right of all, but a privilege offered only a select few. The wife looks this way and that way. She is scanning the apartment, as if memorizing exits, the door to the hallway, the windows that lead to the small lip of a balcony with its intricate ironwork railing. The husband is tense and tightly coiled like a Bengal mother tiger about to strike. He is ready to pounce at whatever comes through the door, to defend his charges.

"Auntie-ji, my dear friend. My dear, dear friend. Of course we will help you." His hand is against his chest, a brace to keep his heart from falling out. "It is not safe for you to live here, anymore." Then, he wanders to the door, and checks the new bolt my kindly neighbour has bought and installed for me. He wanders down the hall and into each room, closing and latching all the windows and drawing shut all my lace curtains. It will not help, but his actions make me smile.

"What if your attackers return? We must report this to the police," the wife says. She stands up and walks towards me. Her right foot crunches small pieces of the vase still littering the floor, while her left foot accidentally sends a piece skittering into the corner. Distracted, she follows its motion, as if hypnotized, and then stoops and begins to collect each fragment one by one.

*

I had never realized that India could be such an erotic experience till we rode the train to Agra to visit that mausoleum to love, the Taj Mahal. The train we boarded was rust-coloured with a single yellow plume running down its length. From the platform, I had made out the white letters spelling "Ladies Compartment" in English. "Oh, a ladies compartment! I think I might like to try that!" I told my husband. We had argued a bit, and then the train started. I trotted alongside the way I had seen a woman in front of me do, and then the smiling women inside reached out to pull me on board, too. I leaned out and waved to my husband, urging him to board the next compartment.

The ladies compartment was packed, and as the train swayed, we were all spooned together, collectively holding each other up by lack of any space to fall. Someone's Buddha belly fit nicely into the curve of my back, and someone's spongy breast pressed shyly up against my arm. Saris swished and slithered all around me. A teenager's fluffy hair tickled my lips. As we moved from station to station, I tried to form the words to describe the experience, tried to see the words on an imaginary page, but they were in a foreign script, a beautifully ornate calligraphy. The experience was untranslatable, in the same way that there are no words to describe floating in water or watching your baby crown from your body. I was quite pleased with my little adventure, but Mo was ticked off when we disembarked.

"The ladies compartment is for women travelling alone — working women and schoolgirls. You're not alone. You're with me. The regular compartment is perfectly safe with a male escort."

"I want to see India through my own eyes, not just through yours, can you understand?" I tried to explain the strange impulse that had overtaken me.

When we arrived at the Taj Mahal, my husband trailed far behind me as I padded barefoot across the marble floors after Rohan, our earnest tour guide with the slicked back hair who catalogued for us Shah Jahan's love for Mumtaz in the yellow marble, jasper and jade inlays on the walls, the calligraphy, and the lattice work so intricate it looked like lace. I clutched my stomach with one hand and reached my other hand for my husband's when Rohan told us that Mumtaz, Shah Jahan's third wife, had died tragically in childbirth — I was thinking of our home now empty with our daughter gone to Hawaii to study, and my womb, vacuumed cleaned after our last sorry miscarriage — but my husband kept both hands to himself, deep in his pockets, and jingled his change rudely. And so it was not he, but I, who cried upon hearing the translation of the inscription, Shah Jahan's own words:

"Should guilty seek asylum here, Like one pardoned, he becomes free from sin. Should a sinner make his way to this mansion, All his past sins are to be washed away. The sight of this mansion creates sorrowing sighs; And the sun and the moon shed tears from their eyes.

The Delhi train station is a maze almost impossible to navigate. We are misdirected countless times and then made to step over rail after rail to get to the correct platform, while, sometimes a hair's breadth away, trains huff and puff and threaten to mow us down. It is the stuff of nightmares, to lift one's foot over one silver rail and then another, never knowing from which direction the train will charge at us.

Nothing stops Miss Kamla Vati from her task, not the old white buffalo crossing in front of her, not the cats chasing mice and bits of paper floating in the wind, or the one-legged beggar who shakes his tin tumbler in our faces. No, Miss Kamla Vati is a hunched gnome forging forever forward, using her umbrella as a walking stick. I'm finding it hard to keep up. I tell myself, she is not real. She is a character in a story I haven't yet written. If I were in my writing studio, I would write her into being. I would describe her as a hunched gnome, forging forever forward. I would describe the cats chasing bits of paper floating in the wind. Suddenly, I miss my studio — not the magazine deadlines, the pleading for extensions, but the space of my studio, the space that says "I am here. Here, I can be anything I want. I can be a mother. I can be a woman who has never had children. I can be a cowboy, a member of the IRA, a police officer in the Bronx."

I feel faint. It's all the sugary drinks, bottles and bottles of Fanta Orange to combat the heat. My shoes are stiff with Delhi grime. I wish I had not declined Mo's offer to drop me off at the hotel. He had mumbled something about our coming too soon after the last miscarriage, but I wasn't sure if his concern was routine or genuine or just a way to be rid of me for a short while.

"Here it is, the correct platform. Mind your feet." Miss Kamla Vati is calling to me as I step up from the rail corridor onto yet another low platform crowded with passengers waiting for their train.

My husband holds out his hand to me, but I decline. The lady is formidable, to have survived what she has, and I don't want her to think I'm like the laced up Victorian ladies of yesteryear, the memsahibs dropping into dead faints in the heat.

The train we are waiting for arrives five minutes late. We watch its disgorgement: men in three piece suits, in flopping *kurta* pajamas, a few in short-sleeved shirts and blue jeans, fewer still in sarongs. They hop from the metal lip of the train to the concrete platform. We have to cut a swath through them to search for the ladies compartment. Mohammed walks tight against me, clutching my arm possessively. Still, men use the excuse of the crowd to brush up against me. I feel a hand brush my breast, one pinch my bottom. I don't tell Mohammed. I translate the pinch into words. Sharp, as if someone were cutting out a piece of my flesh with a knife. I see my words bloody on a white page. The font is big and fat with outrage, the lettering taking up half the space. I've read about eve-teasing, that this type of sexual violence is the norm here, but I'm not sure what Mohammed, with his indiscriminate boxer's fist and ever-throbbing amygdala, would do if I told him the sad fact that even as he walks beside me, he can't protect me.

I notice the women look as I feel, wary of men, their bodies contracting to avoid touch. Most have male escorts, a brother, a father, an uncle, a husband. The women are adorned and beautiful, flesh peeking out seductively from folds of cloth draped artistically over their frames. There's the glitter of their gold, the sparkling brilliance of the glass bangle sheaths that encircle their forearms. I want to speak to them, ask them a million questions. I would start with the woman in a peacock blue sari accompanied by a barrel-chested man in a grey business suit who had pinched me nonchalantly as he walked by. I would ask her naughty questions about her husband, her sex life, her bargains with life.

The old lady pulls a piece of white cardboard from her big boat of a purse from the fifties. I can recognize the markings on it as Urdu. She holds the makeshift sign aloft, high above her head, so the women disembarking can see it. We are looking for a thirteen-year-old girl with a first and last name that rhyme. But the only children on board are with their mothers.

A middle-aged lady in a blue sari is fussing with the clasp of her cloth suitcase. Miss Kamla Vati pokes a knotty index finger into her shoulder to get her attention. "Any girls travelling alone?" she asks in English, pointing inside.

The woman is from the south and speaks a language voluptuous with vowels, but a smattering of Hindi, too. My husband translates the Hindi for me, but I can read the answer for myself in the shrug of her shoulders. His breath is hot on my neck, and he is standing entirely too close, but this is India, and we are all scrunched together everywhere we go. I'm starting to get used to it.

Miss Kamla Vati and my husband confer in Kashmiri, huddled together, co-conspirators. He hoists the old woman onto the step and she disappears into the compartment. Through the open windows we hear her calling the girl's name, her voice trailing as she moves farther and farther away from us, yet I still feel the need to whisper to my husband on the platform.

"Are you sure we have the right train?" I ask.

"Absolutely sure."

"Perhaps she never left home, changed her mind instead? Or maybe Miss Kamla Vati just mixed it up. She is pretty old, after all."

"Maybe."

"What do we do now?"

"We'll wait with her for the next train."

"Oh, Mo, must we?" I'm tired and want to strip off my soaked and grimy *salwar kameez* and take a cool shower at our suite at the Oberoi. I wanted time to dot some sandalwood perfume behind my ears, reapply the kohl around my eyes and put on my new white lace bra. I had hoped for a nice dinner together, a romantic evening alone, some makeup sex. It had been five weeks since the procedure, and I was starting to feel like myself again, and wanted to spread my legs and share that with him.

"You can always take a taxi back to the hotel."

The gruff tone in his voice makes me realize he has not forgiven me my earlier trespass, for travelling without him on the train to Agra. "No. That's okay. I'll wait here with you," I say, trying to placate him.

We have always been a team in the past.

The platform is nearly empty now. I hear the chug of another train arriving on a distant platform, the dull roar of traffic circling the roundabout, the sharp bleats of Vespa and auto-rickshaw horns, the tired cry of a tea-wallah making his rounds, selling chai. Background sounds, sounds you could fall asleep to. I take a handkerchief out of my purse and mop my forehead and pat my neck. I would like to swipe it across my breasts where the sweat is itching my skin, but it would be considered immodest. I wish I had some water to drink. I put my head on my husband's shoulder.

"All this waiting" my husband says, "always this waiting."

"What do you mean?"

He sweeps his arm to encompass the railway station. I think he means the girl who has not arrived, but then he sweeps his arm to encompass the sky, then me. It's as if he's playing charades with me, and I have to decipher the meaning of this large and all encompassing gesture. When he sweeps his arm to encompass my belly, I finally understand.

"It'll all work out fine," I try to reassure him. "I still have more time. I'm only forty-two, after all."

He's pacing back and forth on the platform, looking up at the windows to see if he can spot Miss Kamla Vati. He stops suddenly, and laughs and laughs, doggy little yaps, then leans a hand onto the train for support, as if he's just run ten miles and is trying to catch his breath. "I'm not sure I can do this anymore." He wipes his eyes, puts a hand through his hair.

Here we go again, I think. "What are you saying?"

Rosemary Hammond, our fertility counselor, warned me of this in her office stuffed with velvet pillows and Kleenex boxes, a dreamcatcher catching dreams in the window and a gigantic crystal tucked under her chair, for clarity, she said. She warned me that my husband's grief might spring up in unexpected ways. Like I didn't know that. I told her, "Mohammed always laughs when he's upset, it's just his way."

"I don't think I can do this anymore." He puts his head in his hands. I have an urge to ruffle his hair, and a competing one to shake him.

"But we've come all this way. All this way, Mo!" Suddenly, I feel as if I'm trying to bring a kite down in stormy weather, and the wind is fighting to snatch it away. "We've spent all this money on in vitro, on the drugs, on all those quacks. We can't stop now." The midday sun is reflecting off the metal and glass surfaces of the train, so much so that I feel lit up from inside, translucent, like a deep-sea fish, like everyone can see my insides. I notice people on the platform are staring at us.

"We have waited and waited for a child who has never arrived, but we have neglected to see that others need our help." He points to the train.

I shake my head in confusion. This is not just grief, I think. "What are you saying?" My head is spinning. I don't care if people are watching. I hit his chest with my hands, my eyes closed tight. Only Mo can bring me this quickly to tears.

He holds my fists away from his chest. His large hands are manacles, I am always a prisoner to his whims: midnight grocery runs for chocolate ice-cream; day trips to the country to find a pond — not just any old pond, a pond with lilies; and now this sudden trip to Ireland and India.

"I think I might like to stay here for a while."

"Here?" I know better, but my eyes scan the train station looking for "here."

"In India."

"India? You want to stay in India?" I don't understand what he is saying, and for a moment, I wonder if he's even speaking English, and not Hindi or Kashmiri, or any of the other 52 dialects of India.

"Yes. With Miss Kamla Vati."

As if on cue, Miss Kamla Vati, steps out of the shadow of the train to stand in the bright Delhi sunlight before us.

"Look. Look at her," my husband whispers.

I look at Miss Kamla Vati, the modern day Indian version of Harriet Tubman. She is oblivious to our domestic quarrels, as if our problems are so tiny she can't see them, enclosed as they are in the dark closet of our private grief. Her quarrels are with the larger map of the world. *Her quarrels are with the larger map of the world,* I translate my thoughts into words on the page, and they are thin and spidery, as if all the hope in the world had leaked out of them.

"She is not on board," Miss Kamla Vati says, her face grim. "We'll just have to send a telegram to check the girl's departure from Jammu, then." She shakes her head slowly. She is dejected, but determined. "In the meantime, we will wait here, just in case she arrives on the next train. Let us hope for the best."

It's strange but Miss Kamla Vati appears to be trembling, her body undulating in the vapours of the heat rising all about us. There's a dizzy-making vibration under the soles of my feet, like a thousand wild horses stampeding. The trains are coming, I think, trains rumbling through this corridor from one place to another, one moment to the next, bringing one life to another, taking one life away from another. And just as I fall into a faint, I feel the platform opening up beneath my feet, and I feel myself break through to somewhere unrecognizable, somewhere not on any known map.

*

In my nightmares, there is a man, but the man won't go to the mountain, so the mountain hikes up its sari, reveals its delicate ankles and comes to him. Sometimes, the mountain does not come, but the man is clever. He is an engineer. He knows how to make the mountain come to him. He blows up the mountain, and the mountain falls into his hands. I am the man in my dream. I am the man in real life. When I put a piece of the mountain to my lips, I smell chocolate, but taste dynamite.

"I miss Kashmir," I said to Miss Kamla Vati when we first took up our perch on her damaged dining room chairs. "I miss my mountain."

"The Kashmir you know is gone," she said, her tone matter-of-fact.

I listened with a heavy heart as she tells me that the house I grew up in, a wooden house by a river lined with willows and poplars in the pine-scented, *chenar*-filled mountains, is a bombed out ruin. The villagers of my tiny hamlet have all fled to live in corrugated tin shacks along the river Tawi, or one-room cement block tenements in refugee camps outside Jammu and across the border in Azad Kashmir.

The tourists no longer come to gawk at the Hanging Gardens. They don't stroll around the perimeter of Dal Lake, the lake my father poled his donga along, selling bitter gourd and other green vegetables in the floating market, or rent a shikara and float on the lotus-strewn lake with its fishy, mossy smell of decaying leaves. No, the lake is no longer alive with boats, long and pointy like delicate shoes, tourists peeking out from under their canopies to bleach their faces in the sun. Now, the *shikharas* and *dongas* are fidgety, all lined up at the wooden dock tugging at their leashes in the lapping waves. Their once colourful signs announcing their fancy names, their fancy prices, in Hindi, Urdu, English, are fading. When now the dabchicks with their stunted wings flit among the lily pads, when frogs jump from twig to twig into the reed-filled lake or a kingfisher dives for trout, there's no one to point it out and exclaim, to snap a picture.

"The wind carries only the sound of gunfire," Miss Kamla Vati said, "and the smell of petrol fires."

I think of all the things Miss Kamla Vati said about Kashmir, my home, as I scoop my headstrong wife in my arms and call a porter to summon a taxi. My wife is heavy in my arms and a large crowd is forming around us. Miss Kamla Vati wipes Molly's forehead with the *pallou* of her sari.

"She's very hot," Miss Kamla Vati says, concerned. "Has she been sick recently?"

"It's only the weather. She's not used to it."

"I must stay here," Miss Kamla Vati says, apologetically, "to await the girl. But you should take her to the hotel immediately."

An elderly man, his voice hoarse from smoking *bidis*, his teeth red from chewing paan, appeals to the crowd for a doctor. I'm embarrassed at all this attention for a little fainting. No one would make such a fuss on the streets of Toronto. There, my wife's freckles, pale skin and red hair are unremarkable; here, she's a ghost of the colonial past fallen at their feet.

A young woman in a short tunic and white jeans navigates her way through the crowd towards us.

"I'm a doctor. I can look at her, if you'd like." She has caramel-coloured skin freckled with moles, and there is a spiky cut to her hair. I recognize a British accent. She's a tourist from abroad, though she's from here, too.

I nod, and put my wife down on the ground, gently. She is half sitting, propped up against my knees. I keep my hand on her shoulder to stop her from falling over.

"Luvvie, luvvie, can you hear me?" The doctor checks my wife's pulse and lifts her eyelids, then rattles off a series of questions at me. "Any medical problems? Diseases? Heart problems?"

"No. No. No."

The doctor's eyes flick back and forth from me to my wife, to her rounded belly.

"Is she pregnant?"

"No."

"Are you sure?"

"My wife cannot bear any more children," I tell the doctor firmly, but I feel the bite of guilt as if I'm betraying my wife, her tender trust, as I finally say aloud what I've thought all along. To my embarrassment, Miss Kamla Vati has heard me, and is casting sympathetic glances my way.

"Oh," the doctor says, disappointed, as if she had hoped for more of a challenge, as if her backpack contained her stainless steel surgical instruments and she was just looking for an opportunity to slice someone open. "Then there's no cause for worry. My best guess is heatstroke. Some water and cold compresses should revive her."

The woman gets up from her kneeling position. She folds her hands in a namaste of goodbye before rejoining her fellow travellers, short- and long-haired women wearing the hybrid uniform of girls travelling through the subcontinent — blue jeans and long *kameez*. They lug heavy, bulging backpacks, but they are light with the freedom to wander and roam. They remind me of my daughter, of her lust for wandering that has taken her away from us. I have an urge to run after the young doctor, to follow her onto her train, just to see where she would go.

But Molly is coming to, making small snuffling noises. She taps my foot with her hand, and I turn all my attention on her.

"Mohammed?" my wife says, as if she's unsure of whose foot she is tapping. I lean forward, close to her face so I can hear what she is saying.

"I'm so embarrassed. Can you take me to the hotel, please?" She clutches my arm as she tries to stand up.

In the car, my wife clings to me and buries her head in my chest. Her hands stroke my own, absentmindedly. We're snug in the back of a black beetle taxi, but the road to our five-star hotel is full of five-star potholes. The driver darts scornful glances at us in the rearview mirror as he swerves back and forth, tearing us apart, flinging us against the side doors, as if trying to eject us. We are exhausted from the effort it takes just to stay upright in our seats.

"Where's Miss Kamla Vati?" Molly asks.

"She's still waiting for the girl. I'll leave you at the hotel, and then go back to her."

She starts to cry, huddled in the corner of the cab. "Oh, Mo. What was that all about back there? Are you leaving me? Did you bring me all the way to India to leave me?"

"I'm not leaving you, how can you think such a thing?" I am shaken that her thoughts have led her to this conclusion. Molly deserves an explanation, but I'm not sure I have a clear one to give. "Haven't you ever felt your life needed to change direction?" I stop and start uncertainly. "That there is something left unfinished, some debt you need to repay?"

Molly stops crying. It has always bothered me, this ability of hers to start and stop tears, seemingly on a whim. She points her finger at me, jabs the air. "I know that coming here has stirred up lots of feelings. I can see it in you. It was the same for me when we went to Belfast, when I saw my mother again after twenty years. But when we were there, did I abandon you? Did I go off half-cocked on some crazy project thinking I could fix everything that I had ever done wrong, to make amends to everyone and everybody? No, I didn't! When your whole past is screaming at you like that, it's just not the time to be making big life decisions."

I shake my head. Molly doesn't understand.

"Doesn't Miss Kamla Vati have her own family to take care of her? She is not your grandmother, not your aunt. Why must it be you? You have your own family to take care of. What kind of hold does she have over you?" Her last question is a wail.

"You could stay in India with me," I say, but Molly has stopped listening, her head buried in the crook of her arm.

I am torn. I don't know what to do, where I'm needed most. I love Molly, my wife, and I miss Kashmir, even if Kashmir has miscarried its dreams.

When I return to the train station, Miss Kamla Vati is conferring with the stationmaster. A telegram has already been sent to the girl's village.

"How is your wife?" she asks, concerned.

"She is recovering, but we should get you home. You are not looking that well yourself."

Miss Kamla Vati dismisses my concern with the wave of her hand. "There has been report of a bus accident due to a landslide. We are not sure if the girl was on that particular bus, or the one after it. The roads are always treacherous, but more so with the monsoons. It will be a while before the way is cleared again."

We are silent for a moment, lost in our silent remembrances of Kashmir roads, of heart-stopping rides down the zigzagging mountain, the mountain road with no fences to keep the endless drop at bay, the rusted carcasses of cars unlucky enough to have fallen off the edge.

Miss Kamla Vati pats my arm, as if I am the one who needs comfort, but I can see she is very worried, too. Her brow is furrowed, and her left eyelid flutters madly. I hold my arm out to her and she allows me to navigate us a path out of the train station while porters in red jackets swarm, begging for a chance to tote our non-existent luggage on their cloth-wrapped heads.

The gatekeeper is annoyed that he must open the gate for us, though it is his job. "All this coming and going, this toing and froing," he says, under his breath. He spits on the road before closing the gate to the compound — a red-flecked gob of wet mashed up paan. He calls after us, "Where is your new visitor?" His tone is mocking.

"She has not yet arrived," Miss Kamla Vati explains.

"I have slipped a telegram under your door," he says, with a smirk. "Perhaps it will explain the problem."

Miss Kamla Vati thanks him, but I would like to smack him. In fact, I make a mental note to have a talk with him after I leave Miss Kamla Vati for the night. She is much too polite for her own good. I feel it's my duty to help her find a new place to live, whether she wants to go or not.

I help her open her door, and we enter the apartment, kept cool with its drawn curtains and shuttered windows. I hear the crunch of something, like fine sand under my sandals.

Miss Kamla Vati flicks on the light switch, and the overhead bulb hums as it wakens. Its yellow spotlight reveals the three-legged table, the torn divan, the dents and black shoe prints on the walls and, on the floor, the telegram. I snatch it up off the polished concrete floor and hand it to Miss Kamla Vati.

"Read it to me, please," she asks, giving it back to me. "My eyes ... I can't see too well in this light."

It's a two-line telegram with sentences half coughed out, full of stops and starts. It is as puzzled as we are as to the status of the girl. *Left Jammu yesterday. To arrive 2 p.m. today. Please notify on arrival. All concerned.*

"I'm sure she will arrive on the next train. I'll wait for it tomorrow," Miss Kamla Vati says doggedly.

"Is that wise? You are not even sure what train she will be on. What would be the point in waiting?" I'm sad for Miss Kamla Vati, for her broken down house, for her charge, the girl who is missing. Miss Kamla Vati, though, is not sad for herself.

She looks at me perturbed. "But what else is there to do?"

The gatekeeper gives me a mocking bow as I exit the compound.

I turn around and shout, "What is your problem?" I stick out my foot to stop the gate he's trying to close. But the force of my foot kicks the gate open, and it hits the gatekeeper on his forehead with a soft thud.

He looks up at me dazed and surprised, but his hands block his face reflexively in anticipation of blows.

I notice how emaciated he looks, his arms thin and ropy. His body bent in on itself, as if he's sheltering his heart deep in the cave of his body because there's nowhere else safe for it to be.

"There's no problem, no problem," he simpers.

I feel sickened by what I have done, at how I have reduced a grown man to the responses of a cowering dog. But I can't let it go. "You will not bother Miss Kamla Vati again," I order.

He nods, straightens his shirt, pulls on his *lungi*, coughs nervously into his hands.

They are the hands of a skeleton. "You're practically starving!" I'm dismayed at how long it has taken me to realize this, his obvious vulnerability. I give him all the money I have except for what I need to get back home.

I am tired of all the fighting. It is as if the conflict in Kashmir has played out, not just in the verdant and lake-filled valleys, but in my mind. And without my awareness, my brain has been seeking out a solution, like it sometimes does with an engineering challenge — the hydraulics of a dam, or the problem of not enough pressure in pipes — one that ties both Miss Kamla Vati and the gatekeeper's survival together with the diaphanous thread of self-interest and mutual gain. The best I can hope for is a temporary peace.

"I will send you money each month, care of Miss Kamla Vati, so long as she is safe and alive."

When I return to the hotel, my wife has already packed. Somehow she has obtained a rail pass, and she waves it under my nose. There's nothing for me to do but to accompany her to the train station. She insists on boarding the ladies compartment. It doesn't make any sense to me, her insistence on travelling the rails all about Southern India without me.

"We need a break. It's better this way," she says. She doesn't look me directly in the eye, but when a group of women pass her by, she smiles shyly at them. "There's so much to see in India," she says.

I hear myself whine. "What about us? Will you be coming back to

Delhi? To me?"

She is only half paying attention to me. The train has started, and she is looking for that gap to jump into.

"Molly," I say, grabbing her arm. "Don't go."

She unhooks my hand from her arm. "Nothing's working out as planned, Mo. We came to see Kashmir and to try again to have a baby. But nothing has worked out, has it?"

"What?" I say, petulantly, though I know perfectly well what she means and what an ass I have been. I have been ready to blow my family apart, to hold on to ... what?

"We came for two things, but now we are doing something altogether different, aren't we?"

I'm not sure if she's referring to me or to herself.

The train snorts its way into position beside us and Molly climbs the step, turning at the top to say goodbye. "Stay with Miss Kamla Vati. Take care of her, if you want. I don't really understand why you are doing what you are doing, but it's admirable of you to help her."

"I have done my duty by her now. It's done. All over." I follow her up the metal stairs. "Please don't go." It's my turn to cry. And I spread out the red carpet of my love to her, burying my face in her neck and whispering endearments into her ear as I have each night for the last twenty years: *my ras malai, my sweet jalebi, my bulbul.* But my words are no longer the soft hooks that have pulled her sweetly into my arms all these years. She's off, the train slowly shuffling away before gaining speed. There's nothing for me to do but to wait for my mountain to come back to me.

THE TIN BUS

I AM TRAPPED IN THE NO. 52. A LANDSLIDE OF SLICK BROWN EARTH has knocked askew and then toppled our bus, like a tin toy in the hands of an angry child. Through the twisted steel rim of the smashed window, I can see the Himalayas outside still threatening to fall on me. Other passengers, the driver, even a bent old woman passing by have stuck their faces against the jagged edges of the mud-splattered window to peer inside. I am the upside-down girl in the upside-down bus, and the cutting smell of diesel wafting in the balmy air has us all alarmed.

"Am I going to die?" I ask the ones outside. Never more than now have I wanted an honest answer to this question.

I was born with a disease of the blood that turns my skin as pale as a tourist from the West, my breathing as racked and phlegmy as an old man's, and my limbs as flaccid as a rotting cucumber. On my worst days, I am forced to lie still in my cot and forgo my usual pleasures. I cannot unspool a kite and guide it through the open skies, or skip through the walled city and gather children and lead them into play like a pied piper. I cannot raise my voice to sing a *ghazal* with my cousin Mani as she plays the harmonium, or even move a hand to turn the pages of the books my mother borrows from the schoolteacher next door. When I am incapacitated like this, my mother, too, is im-mobilized, hunched in the parlour room, keening in prayer.

On the good days, days when I am stronger than an elephant, quicker than a tiger, smarter than a cobra, my mother bounces through the streets with her market sack, singing old Hindi film songs, happy. I am the only one in our small family who does not sing when I recover. It is because I know that I am as variable as a generator — one swift kick and I may stop as suddenly as I started.

It is for this reason that I forever needled my mother with my question: Am I going to die? My mother would only turn away to wipe her eyes with the frayed end of her *pallou*. Even Mani, who could be counted on to never lie, pious as she is, would only say, "If it is to be, it is to be."

The doctor, too, ignored my question, colluding with my mother, whispering his prognosis in her ears only. He would dangle his presents, glass medicine bottles with their shiny foil tops, their silver calm, just out of my reach, in an attempt to distract me. I collected these bottles the way Anjali next door collected dolls and even named them after those invested with special powers, those who could change my fate. Genie. *Nagar.* Monsoon. The doctor's visits were sporadic, the frequency depending on my health and our ability to afford the remedy — vitamins mostly, sometimes a blood coagulant. He would administer his shots with finesse, first disinfecting my marred bottom with its array of purple stab wounds with a soft cotton ball, "pleasure," and then jabbing me with the sharp point of his needle, "pain."

A day before my twelfth birthday, I developed an insatiable thirst for the truth as I lay in my string cot, my limbs as useless to me as a tin plate in a famine. With my weakened hand I swiped away the mashed up rice and dhal that hovered near my mouth. I spat at Mani as she read to me from the *Kashmir Times* and, worst of all, I refused to smile for my mother when she wiped me with a rough cloth soaked in rubbing alcohol and turned me over so I would not get prickly bed sores.

My bad behaviour I directly attributed to the schoolteacher who helped me with my English. To appease my voracious hunger for the world outside, she delivered stacks of books for me to read, culled from her prized collection, some of them from abroad, sent by a cousin in Canada. Along with *Aesop's Fables*, the *Ramayana*, Thomas Hardy, the poetry of Tagore and the Sufis, and the writings of Khalil Gibran, she had made the mistake of lending me one on Greek mythology. There I met Proteus, a minor sea god, who had the power of prophecy but who would assume different shapes to avoid answering questions.

At this point, I threw the book on the floor, not caring to read to the end. Was this not my mother, the doctor, my cousin, even the schoolteacher? All who knew my fate, yet refused to tell me the truth? Instead, their eyes wandered in pity over my body, desiccated as fallen wood, rotting in the dry air.

My mother, hearing the thud of the thick book on the cement floor, ran towards me, fearing the worst. Feverish with my sudden anger, I demanded an answer to my question.

"I'm old enough to know!" I shouted.

"What does it matter?" my mother yelled back at me, her voice shrill with frustration.

"It matters!" I said, banging my legs against the bed, thrashing about as best as I could. "Absolutely, it matters."

I thought of all the things I wanted to do before I died. To learn to draw like the miniaturists, to play the harmonium and best Mani, to whisper with Anjali about the romantic entanglements, the sex scandals of our favourite film stars. Knowing when I would die would make it possible to know which to do first, which I might have to give up.

"I only meant, enjoy each day as it comes," my mother said, reaching to stroke my forehead, trying to appease me.

I slapped her hand away. I was inconsolable. The doctor had predicted the schoolteacher's husband's death to the exact month (nine months), and therefore, he must also know how long I had to live, I argued. And so did my mother, I accused. Not everything was a mystery. I just wanted to know, would I live long enough for my chest to strain at the tight fabric of a sari blouse, to carry a satchel and walk through the doors of Jammu College, to take a mustard bath and wrap a wedding *zari* around my waist? Or even just long enough to braid my own hair again, to slip my *chappals* on my own feet, to walk myself to the latrine. I was sure they knew how long I had left in this life. That they refused my request for the truth was unbearably cruel.

Just before my mother handed me my bus ticket and an old bed cloth stuffed with a few of my best *kurta* pajamas, pencils and exercise books for my studies in Delhi, and, sandwiched between two pieces of cardboard, her marriage photo and a few hundred rupees, she said, "I will not let you die." She kissed me on my forehead and forced me to bounce my cross-eyed baby brother about for a few minutes, which I did, in a distracted fashion, and received a slap for my inattention.

"Is this how you say goodbye? Have I not taught you better?" My mother blew her nose on her best white kerchief.

"No, Ma, you have taught me well." I hugged her around her middle and felt the slippery nylon fabric of her sari start to slip from its tight tuck in the cord that held up her petticoat. She didn't seem to notice, her waist jiggling as she sobbed.

Even as I embraced her, I was thinking of the frenetic busy-ness of Delhi, the shiny new glass buildings in the bank district, the sparkling storefront lights, the never-ending line of vendors fronting busy streets selling paper violins, tin toys, jingling bangles and all manner of trinkets. I was thinking of eating as many sweets as I wanted far from my mother's usual prying eyes and heavy slaps. I was not thinking of her refusal to answer the one question that nagged at me and troubled my dreams long after I had recovered.

Yesterday when I emerged from the back courtyard after cleaning my teeth with my neem twig, my mother recoiled at my appearance. My mother was poised to dip the expensive electric coil into the pail to heat my water for my bath (something she only did for me on account of my condition), when she glanced up at the thock-thock of my *chappals* approaching her. The red-hot coil fell onto the concrete floor with a clang and slithered about like an angry serpent before coming to rest a hand's breadth away from my infant brother's feet. I was scratching my itching chest. Overnight, it seemed I had become a woman, my breasts surging against the tightness of my *salwar kameez.*

"Now you are a woman, now you are prey," she said, and bit on her lower lip, shaking her head at my chest.

She was thinking of Wahida, our neighbour, who had been lost. To whom, we did not know. The list of possible culprits was long: the mercenaries girded with grenade belts, who milled about our village with their heavy rifles; the Indian Army who roamed villages with trucks and tanks that flattened scrub and shacks and anything else in its path; and, most frighteningly, the young boys with God in their eyes and acid in their pails. She had been snatched while hanging her mother's saris on the taut line strung between two walnut trees behind their house.

So, today I was put on a bus, headed on its downward slide to Jammu, where I was to board a train to Delhi to stay with the schoolteacher's unmarried great aunt, Miss Kamla Vati, a former vice-principal in a private girl's school.

"You are twelve years old, but if you stay in our village, you will not live long," my mother had said to me as she penned the words to Miss Kamla Vati at the telegraph office. She had flinched as the bitter irony of her words dawned on her. Usually, her sadness flowed around me like a river while I stood on a sandbank untouched by the waters, but today I felt its cool wetness, and for once I did not get angry. My mother was thinking not of my disease, but of the other ways in which lives were snatched. Already, collecting wood for our fire or herding our goats up the mountain had taken my father and my father's youngest brother, my mother's uncle and several of my cousins. Luckily, the schoolteacher had said in an attempt to console my mother, we were a large family.

"Land mines, ambushes, stray bullets, random executions — they cannot kill us all," the schoolteacher next door once yelled across the courtyard, defiant, as we slammed our windows and doors shut in submission to the curfew laws.

"Everything has a cycle," she proclaimed. "Empires rise, then they fall. Rome fell, as did the Ottoman Empire. Did we not kick the British out? Everything has a cycle. We are born, then we die. We are healthy, we are sick. We feel defeated, then we are hopeful. Nothing lasts forever. You'll see, our home will one day again be that peaceful place where the doe and the tiger can drink from the same pond." Then she pulled her front door shut, and we heard her heavy metal bolt slide into its accustomed place.

What is a life worth? My life has been nothing but a heavy sack on my mother's back. My illness has scarred her forehead with worry lines and whittled her fat away with the constant work of hefting and hauling my body around. It has robbed her of the last of my father's rupees hoarded in the tin box of her *almirah*, and of her inheritance; she has had to become an alchemist, transforming her gold bangles and necklaces into medicine bottles.

I have held so much anger against my mother, so much contempt for her refusals to speak the truth, and yet my unhappiness pales beside her own. A widow left alone to fend for herself after my father was blown to pieces, burdened with a sickly child and a new baby; had she not sacrificed everything for me?

About to mount, one foot placed on the steps of the brightly painted bus, I hesitated, awash with newfound respect and admiration for my mother. Then I thought to ask, "What about Mani, will she come soon?"

"We can only afford to send one away at this time, and it must be you. If they come to ransack our house again or if the trouble worsens," she said, clutching her hand against her chest, "how could any of us flee if you were here in your sick bed?"

She added, "I will not let you die."

I hold on to the last words my mother said to me. As she has deemed that I will not die, I cannot bring myself to contradict her. It is hard to reconcile this promise with the sad fact of my situation at present on this wrecked bus. It is for this reason that I hover, trying to find a remedy to my situation.

The tired, red-eyed driver was just one of the dangers we accept in our part of the world. The slippery monsoon-washed strip of a road, another. And land mines, ambushes, floods, yet others.

My mother had followed me onto the bus before it chugged down the mountain. She sat me opposite an elderly couple returning from wedding festivities, festivities that went on despite the curfews. They were strangers, but had nodded at my mother's anxious face and agreed to keep an eye out for me.

"*Beti,* you listen to Uncle and Auntie," my mother had warned me, slapping my face, gently this time, the better to imprint on me her message. I had been staring at the chicken in a cage being readied to be strapped to the top of the bus. The bird had been marked with yellow paint on its right wing, and I wondered at its meaning.

My mother left abruptly then. The bus driver revved his engine and we were off. I waved to my mother, who clutched her *pallou* about her nose, perhaps against the black stench of the exhaust, or perhaps because she was sobbing.

To distract me, Uncle handed me a small packet of sweetmeats across the aisle, which I accepted with thanks. It was only then that I noticed the other passengers on the bus.

In front of me was a hippie, his face abraded by long-ago chicken pox scars, his wheatish hair in a long ponytail at the back. He held his shiny metal camera out the window and clicked at ten-second intervals, too scared to poke his head out to look at the drop below.

I could hear the camera whizzing when he had finished a roll of film. It was electronic and silver and I longed to have a look at it. He had said only a few words to me after I boarded: *Namaste* and *May I take your picture?* I allowed him to point his camera at me as I stood stiffly in the aisle, holding my cloth bag, holding my breath, hoping no one would report back to my mother that I had conversed with a hippie.

Several rows behind me sat an African man who looked very much like the Kenyan who had just been traded into India's soccer league. I had seen his picture in the newspaper as I passed by the vendor at the market. He shared the thinly padded green vinyl seat with a man in a silk *kurta* and jeans, a silver thermos on his lap of a brand not found in India. It made me wonder if he was an Indian living abroad. His arm was draped over the back of the seat, as if he and the Kenyan soccer player were close friends. I wondered what they were doing so far from Delhi where the team practised in the Olympic Park. Nobody travelled into Kashmir anymore, except the Indian Army, people's relatives, a trickle of tourists misled by greedy tour operators and, sometimes, wary reporters clutching ID cards and riding in jeeps escorted by the army.

The bus was almost empty, which was not uncommon for this time of year, just at the beginning of monsoon season. The road to

Jammu zigzagged all the way down the mountain. One side, a wall of mountain, the other side, emptiness. Below, the rusting carcasses of cars, trucks and buses.

"Just don't look down," the Indian living abroad said to his friend who had dared to poke his shiny, bald head out the open window, only to gulp at the view.

"This might be a good time to get religion," he added, joking. He patted the soccer player on his back reassuringly. "It's better if you don't look out. Why don't you read your book?"

"Trade seats, then?" The soccer player moved to get up and after a bit of push and shove and laughing they switched seats.

The bus moved along the dirt road like a woman with blisters on her feet, hesitant. What I saw from my window: the crumbly wall of brown earth, the very shoulder of the mountain, then the next minute, at the hairpin turn, the edge of the road and the drop into the emptiness of a sky without reference points, no tree, no house, nothing to give it meaning. I was on the edge of the world. I stopped looking down, turning my gaze forward. That's when I saw, through the driver's window and its layer of dust, a tiny Sherpa ahead of us, straining under her heavy load of wood, guiding her goats along the mountain road up to Sanasar where the shepherds meet.

The hippie stood and stuck his stringy body through the window to snap a picture.

"Such a hard life she has," Uncle said to me, but in English, so that the foreigners could understand. "Not much to eat on the mountain." He shook his head sadly.

The foreigners glanced at the woman, her back bent with the heavy weight of the gnarled old twigs, her firewood. She had stopped to readjust the load on her back. I could see her grimace with the effort. The Indian living abroad pointed her out to his friend, who stood up to see her better.

"I see her," the soccer player exclaimed.

"Wow, I didn't know a woman could be a Sherpa!" the hippie said.

"Not just a profession. Also a people," Uncle explained, his English words slow and deliberate so that the hippie could understand him.

"The Sherpa, as you know them, are a creation of the leisure class. Sherpas were a people, a tribe, a group, mostly shepherds, before some became guides for the foolhardy trekkers," the Indian living abroad clarified.

"Cool."

"Not so cool," the Indian living abroad continued. "Because of the war, no more trekking here. No more livelihood. Her way of life is going fast. She's a ghost. Everything now is exports, silicon chips, satellite televisions and American videos."

Uncle added, "All this fighting, heavy tanks and blasting is destroying the mountain. That is why the Sherpas pray to mountain gods."

"Yes," the Indian living abroad said, "the two greatest lies ever told: that Columbus discovered America, and that Hillary was the first person to set foot on the summit of Everest."

"Certainly, there are more than two," the soccer player said, raising his eyebrow, and the Indian living abroad, the hippie and Uncle laughed in unison.

Then it started to rain; silver rivulets ran down the glass window, blurring our vision. Water sprayed us through the open windows. The Indian living abroad stood up to slide his window closed.

"Poor woman, see how she suffers," Uncle said, his eyes as wet as the woman outside.

An army jeep honked behind us. Our bus driver swerved, and pulled as far as he dared against the wall of the mountain to let the convoy pass.

I could see directly into the back of the jeep as they passed, an army general, a row of ribbons on his chest, and a small worried looking man beside him, clutching a doctor's bag.

"Usually, they provide escort," the driver said, over his shoulder. "For safety," he added. "Now, they are busy-busy. Something big they must be planning."

I fell asleep, one side of my face pressed against the cool surface of my window. Perhaps it was the rain pattering on the roof, the wipers ticking like a metronome, the hypnotic thrumming of the engine that caused me to drift into sleep. Or perhaps it was the excitement of the day, the agony of separation from my mother without whom I had never spent a day, not even when hospitalized (she would sleep in a cot next to mine and minister to me, for which the overworked nurses were grateful). As the distance crept between us, her at the top of the mountain, me slipping to the bottom, I regretted my bouts of anger, the way I used to turn my cheek away from her lips seeking to kiss me goodnight, the thousand other petty ways I had snubbed her. I did not hear the heavy curtain of mountain close around us. I did not hear the curse of the red-eyed driver as he stood up to heft all his body weight onto the brake lever, trying to stop the bus from slipping on the wet muck oozing down the mountain onto the narrow ribbon of our road.

I woke because I heard praying. I thought I was once again at home, woken in the morning by the low rumble from the mosque on the hill, praises to Allah amplified by loud speakers, or by the eerie chanting of women at their home altars doing their morning puja. It was Uncle and Auntie in the seat next to mine praying at the darkness behind the grime of their window as the mountain continued to advance upon us. "*Hai Rama, Hai Rama.*"

"Shit. Shit. Shit," I heard the hippie cry. He was cowering, backed up against the side of the bus.

The soccer player was the first to react. "Open the door," he screamed at the driver's back, as he lunged down the aisle towards the front.

A thud. A torrent of mud engulfed us, darkening our windows to night. The bus lurched this way and that way, pushed and pulled in the slippery river. The driver struggled to keep hold of the steering wheel that was spinning of its own accord in his hands. I tried to brace myself against the seat in front of me the best I could. The roof of our bus cratered. Small rocks, then larger boulders were shelling it, denting the roof, the sides. I covered my head with hands, sure that I would be crushed, and was immediately thrown to the floor for my efforts. Finally, with a big bang, the bus jolted to a stop.

The passengers collected themselves from the floor.

The bus lay perpendicular to the road, its nose crumpled, facing the mountain as if meaning to find a tunnel through it. When I looked back, I could see the rear hung over the edge of the road, the back wheels no more than a few inches from the endless drop.

"For God's sake, let us out!" the soccer player shouted at the stricken driver, who was picking himself up from the front steps. He called back to his friend, "Help me push!"

The Indian abroad limped down the aisle, brushing his hair back in a nervous gesture. Together, they put their weight behind the warped door, straining to push it open. The door creaked and groaned, but it would not budge.

The driver, his face bloody, specks of glass shining on his forehead, shook himself free from his trance, swinging the lever that opened the door, and the two friends toppled outside. The driver then turned towards us, those left on the bus: the cowering hippie, the elderly couple, frozen as the ceramic statutes they prayed to. He shouted to no one in particular, "Get the girl." Then he, too, was gone, leaping out the door.

The Himalayas were not done with us. A second fall of mud tipped the bus over on to its head, then shepherded it as if it were a wayward goat, to the flatness of the hairpin turn. I was knocked unconscious in the tumbling. When I woke, it was difficult to see. My neck was twisted at such an angle that I could peer out the window but glimpse only a portion of the floor. I hung upside down. The green vinyl seat in front of me had crumpled backwards and my chest and waist were pinned against my own seat. I was like a bug being held aloft with pincers. My long braids swished with the slow movements of the bus. I thrashed about trying to free myself from the grip of the seat, gasping for breath, desperate. I could see the trunks and suitcases, bundles of rice and lentils that had once been tied to the top of the bus, now lay strewn about, half submerged in the tide of mud. A speck of white caught my eye. The chicken had been freed of its cage, and it was fighting for footing in the slippery sludge. One wing dangled, broken, and a mantle of mud covered the bird.

There's an old proverb that says as death approaches, even the foolish man becomes wise. It is this that makes the most stubborn man on his deathbed reconcile with the son he has disowned. It is this that makes a murderer confess his crimes, or a miserly, feudal lord leave all his wealth to his long suffering servants. It is this that makes a small-hearted woman gather her children about her and dispense all the love she once forgot to give them.

The stealth of the mountain about to steal my life made me instantaneously wise. I knew that the faces that peered at me from outside the bus would not tell me the truth about my predicament. It was human nature to avoid the truth, as it was human nature to demand it anyway.

"Am I going to die?" I asked the soccer player who hammered at the door that had crumpled closed again in the tumble, then at the front windshield with, first, his bare fists, then a large tin of oil, then a rock. He hammered at the window with whatever he could scavenge amongst the strewn baggage, but there wasn't much to work with.

"Don't worry, we'll get you out," he whispered, determined, even as the glass and metal cut his wrists to the bone and he had to turn back to staunch the flow of blood.

"Am I going to die?" I asked the driver, the only one scrawny enough to attempt to pass through the sole open window, now half buried in mud.

"You should not ask such questions. Can you not see we are trying our best?" he said, as he dived headfirst into the mud, only to reappear still on the outside of the window, spitting mud.

"Am I going to die?" I asked the hippie who lay below me on the ceiling of the bus, his body twisted, the camera strap still around his wrist, its lens pointed at me. But he did not reply.

"Am I going to die?" I asked Uncle whose motionless body, too, lay splayed on the ceiling, having served to break the hippie's fall.

I did not bother asking Auntie, who paced restlessly outside the bus. She had escaped, pulled out by the Indian living abroad just before the landslide of mud toppled the bus. He had re-entered the bus and reached for me, the girl, but Auntie's arms were longer and she clasped on to him for dear life. He hobbled back to the door, jumping into the river of mud with her still pressed to his side. Just before he leapt, he had shouted at me above the rumble, the earth moving, "Little girl, run. Run for the door!"

But I was frozen. Perhaps it was because I had been rudely awoken from my sleep, but I could not differentiate dreaming from the nightmarish drama that swirled about me. And to be truthful, in that moment, I was more fearful of outside with the sky dark as earth, than I was inside the womb of the bus.

Now I could see Auntie's haunted, mud encrusted face, her hands with their knobbly knuckles working at the latches of the windows, calling tonelessly for a husband who would not rise.

"Am I going to die?" I asked, but none would tell me.

The bus started to slide again, imperceptibly at first. With each lurch my rescuers, the driver and the two friends, fell back, giving the river of mud a wide berth, afraid of the slow-moving behemoth. *What else can we do?* I heard them say, wringing their hands.

The bus stopped suddenly, with a sudden knock, as if it had hit a big stone. I could hear the fragile metal of the frame grind against the unforgiving hardness of the rock.

I felt something warm slither down my back and arms. It was blood.

"Ma," I called out, though I knew she wasn't there, outside the bus. "Ma!"

This caused my would-be rescuers to regroup, huddling around each other, gesticulating wildly.

"Nobody travels the road when it's monsoon. We cannot expect travellers here," the driver said, fiddling with his waistband, trying to keep his mud encrusted, soppy pants up.

"What about the army?" the Indian living abroad said, pointing up the mountain. "I saw an army jeep less than half an hour ago."

"They have passed. Unlikely they will return."

"Do you have a radio? A CB radio?" the soccer player said, but the driver shook his head.

Nobody asked for a cellphone. I, myself, had never seen one. I had read in the papers that while the rest of India had been modernizing with cellphones and internet, Kashmir had been forcibly kept in the dark ages; satellite service providers were forbidden to plant their shiny poles and electronic gear here for fear of misuse by the insurgents.

"Husband," Auntie said, and wept.

"How far is the nearest village?" the soccer player said, ignoring her, taking charge.

"Many kilometres away where the road forks. Even then, what could the villagers do? The bus will have plunged over the edge by then. It is no use. It is God's doing."

"Maybe if we could tie a rope around the axle, we could pull the bus away from the edge, out of the mud. We could get her then."

"This is not possible. Look how much the bus is weighing. Look how much mud is inside the bus. We would need ten elephants or three trucks."

"But what about other accidents? What did you do then?"

"Nothing. There is nothing to be done."

And again they resumed their talk of ropes and fulcrums and leverage and lead pipes. Their heads turned away from me, plotting. I was not fooled. In this way, busy with their plans, they would miss the moment they could not bear to witness: the bus slipping over the serrated edge of the road, falling soundlessly till it hit bottom. I was left alone to ponder my fate while I dangled upside down from the ceiling, like a wobbly fan, electricity cut off, about to sputter to a stop.

"It would have been better if she had died quickly," I heard someone say. It was hard to breathe upside down. I felt crushed by my own body weight, and I could feel myself start to slip into unconsciousness.

"How could you say such a thing? She's just a little girl," someone else admonished.

It's the lingering that's difficult for most. I'm sure my rescuers wished they could say, in all honesty, "We jumped out of the bus, but then it fell over the edge. It happened so quickly. There was no time to save the girl, no time to do anything."

No time to do anything, that would have been their only salvation.

I thought of my mother, wondering if she had ever wished me dead, and I knew the answer. As I stared at the stricken faces of my rescuers, I began wishing it myself.

It's the sharp smell of diesel leaking into the balmy air that wakes me.

"There'll be no *deus ex machina* for us," I hear the soccer player say.

My eyes flicker open at his words. He's cradling his head in his bloody hands, his back bent in a posture of defeat. Even he has given up.

His friend nods his head as if he understands, rubbing his back and hiccupping back sobs. The way he says it, I too understand the meaning of the foreign words.

There will be no rescue at the last minute just as the bus is poised to plunge over the edge. Nobody's god or gods could save me now. The world split into two, me on the inside of the tin bus, and on the other, the outsiders, the free ones. Not unlike my bad days, being trapped in my body, unable to even wipe my own nose.

I see the chicken take one last hop, and I see it flutter to freedom, hovering by the drier part of the roadbed, but this does not give me hope. I, who could not believe in anyone's deity, say a prayer for the people on the outside of the tin bus, and then I say a prayer for myself, begging that the answer to my question, "Am I going to die," will be "Yes, but you will not suffer."

A tiny woman appears on the hairpin turn, the woman who had passed us on our way down, the shepherd. Her back is still loaded with twigs, and two goats follow her. The driver ignores her, as do the two men embracing each other for warmth. Only Auntie pulls at her arm, leading her through the mud and pointing inside at me, at her husband below. The shepherd smiles at me, her face lined as a walnut. She retreats to put her bundle down, though Auntie tugs at her to come back.

I smile when she comes back. Why she does I don't know. What can she do, after all?

She puts one foot into the wet and oozing earth and peers at me through the mud-splattered window. She shrugs. "We are all going to die one day," she says to me, though not unkindly.

I start to cry, my tears hot, dripping onto my braids swinging back and forth. The pressure of hanging upside down has rendered me almost blind, and when I blink, little pinpricks of light show through my swollen lids.

"I'll never get to Delhi," I say, and a sudden longing for the city of lights chokes me. "I'll never see my mother again." A fit of hysterics at that last thought overcomes me.

The old woman merely shrugs at my sobs.

Her indifference pains me. "It doesn't matter. I only hope that I die soon," I say, with a resoluteness I don't feel.

The bus starts to sway.

"Perhaps you should stand back," I say, angry at her, and give her a little mocking wave.

I can see the shepherd's eyes widen with fear. I can see her slip and fall face forward in the mud as the bus groans on our thin ledge of a road. I hear the splash her body makes as it plops onto the heavy river of mud, see her struggle to roll her body back onto the solid road. It's like I'm watching a movie and she is Charlie Chaplin sent to entertain me. I almost laugh.

I can hear the bus creaking as it moves, its back end over the edge of the cliff. I know it's time. I'll never again run through the cobbled streets with my favourite yellow kite and call to the neighbourhood children to come and watch me fly. I'll never again fit myself between the pages of a book, and disappear into the velvety lushness of words and other worlds. I'll never again hear the comforting chatter of my infant brother in the next room, as I lie recuperating, nor sun my hair dry on the string cot on our roof and feel the prickly warmth on my skin after the damp coldness of our cement house.

Then I spot two tiny hands clinging to the window, the one the driver had tried to swim through. It's the shepherd, her toothless mouth grim, her face and body covered in mud, a brown apparition. She shoves her body through the small rent of an opening, sliding in to join me, the insider, her arms stretched out to break her fall.

"No." I scream. "Get out." For a moment, I feel a flutter of hope as her body balances at the edge of the window, but what use can her heroics be? Why should she die, too?

She does not waste a second. She flings herself at me, holding onto my arms and using her body weight to pull me free of my pitiless vise. She swings like Tarzan swinging from a vine. I'm released, falling headfirst to the ground with a dull thud. The bus groans and I hold my breath. My knees and wrists and head have hit the ground, and I'm still reeling, but I'm free.

As I emerge from the wreckage, the driver falls to the ground. He hugs me at the knees.

"The gods are great. The gods are good," he weeps.

"But how did you get out?" the soccer player sputters. Then he hugs me, too, enveloping me against him.

"The old woman," I say and shiver. My teeth are chattering but I don't feel cold, his arms and my exhilaration covering me like a warm shawl.

"Auntie saved you?" the Indian living abroad says, incredulous.

"No, the old Sherpa woman with the goats." I point to where she had stood only a minute ago, holding me in her arms, crooning an old lullaby, one my own mother used to sing to me.

She's gone. I search for her, looking down the mountain, up the mountain, even in the mess of the river of mud. She had clambered out of the belly of the bus after me. I had made sure of that. But now she's gone.

"You're imagining things. You must have gotten yourself out," the Indian living abroad says, trying to wipe the blood from the gash on my forehead with a torn piece of his undershirt.

It was a possibility. That I had dreamt her. And then it dawns on me that, if that was true, then it was equally possible that I was dreaming at this very minute, that I was still wedged in the bus, like threads of mango in teeth, impossible to remove, but how a tongue worries it anyway.

It was also a possibility that I had dreamt it all, this life, this dramatic end, just as it was possible that I had lived many lives and this was just one more or one less.

It was possible that the answer to my question had all this time lain inside me like a germinating seed, awaiting the watering of imagination and dreaming.

"Am I going to die?"

"Yes. And many times more."

Fine Fiction from Sumach Press ...

• ON PAIN OF DEATH
Mystery Fiction by Jan Rehner

• SLANDEROUS TONGUE
Mystery Fiction by Jill Culiner

• BOTTOM BRACKET
Mystery Fiction by Vivian Meyer

• THE BOOK OF MARY
A Novel by Gail Sidonie Sobat

• RIVER REEL
A Novel by Bonnie Laing

• REVISING ROMANCE
A Novel by Melanie Dugan

• ROADS UNRAVELLING
Short Stories by Kathy-Diane Leveille

• OUTSKIRTS:
WOMEN WRITING FROM SMALL PLACES
Edited by Emily Schultz

• THE Y CHROMOSOME
Speculative Fiction by Leona Gom

• GRIZZLY LIES
Mystery Fiction by Eileen Coughlan

• JUST MURDER
Mystery Fiction by Jan Rehner
*WINNER OF THE 2004 ARTHUR ELLIS AWARD
for BEST FIRST CRIME NOVEL*

• HATING GLADYS
Mystery Fiction by Leona Gom

• MASTERPIECE OF DECEPTION
Art Mystery Fiction by Judy Lester

• FREEZE FRAME
Mystery Fiction by Leona Gom

Find out more at www.sumachpress.com